Paris, So to Speak

SEAGULL
BOOKS
•
CELEBRATING
40 YEARS

THE GERMAN LIST

NAVID KERMANI

# Paris, So to Speak

Translated by Wieland Hoban

LONDON NEW YORK CALCUTTA

 **GOETHE INSTITUT**

This publication has been supported by
a grant from the Goethe-Institut India.

**Seagull Books, 2023**

First published in German as *Sozusagen Paris* by Navid Kermani
© Carl Hanser Verlag München 2016

First published in English translation by Seagull Books, 2023
English translation © Wieland Hoban, 2023

ISBN  978 1 80309 070 2

Typeset by Seagull Books, Calcutta, India
Printed and bound in the USA by Integrated Books International

Paris, So to Speak

'But not for Jutta.'

I look up at the woman who has put the book on the table for me to sign: early- to mid-forties, I estimate, unusually short, a plain and probably not inexpensive dress, slightly too tight; her body is graceful, though with a little padding around the belly, her smooth blonde hair cut off straight as a ruler at chin height, making her head seem rounder than it is, and her neck is even more delicate, fine as a flower stalk, to use an image my editor will find hackneyed, but a conspicuous number of lines around her brown eyes, I wouldn't call them wrinkles, I suppose one says crow's feet, so older, late forties maybe, yet still girlish; her gaze has a mild, almost sisterly jibe to it, strangely familiar.

'Excuse me?'

'Just make sure you don't write "For Jutta",' the woman reaffirms.

I'm usually confused right after readings, even failing to recognize friends or remember their names. Now too, it takes a while for me to remember the smile that stretches her lips as if in slow motion and makes her cheeks as round as apricots, it takes—I can't judge the time—ten seconds? Fifteen, behind the woman another ten, fifteen people queuing up to get their books signed. The reading went unusually well; without looking up once, I sensed how the audience immersed itself in the story with me, just as I now sense how the people waiting notice my open mouth and restless pupils, my not entirely functional brain, which tries hectically to assign the smile to a particular point in my life and still hasn't registered the nose, which, with its slightly upturned tip, is a sufficiently clear indicator. In the novel from which I read tonight, I compared the bridge of her nose to a ski ramp.

Afterwards, she'll make fun of my confusion, and I'll apologize for being so dense; she'll downplay our love, but I'll insist firmly that I longed for her for 30 years, which is why I wrote more than just a letter: I wrote a whole book. Every day, I'll tell her, every day I hoped to find her reply in the letterbox, and at every reading I looked out for her. But when she's standing in front of me, and even says the name I made up for her, it takes me ten or fifteen seconds to recognize her, long enough for the ten or fifteen people behind her to notice that something's wrong. I finally leap up and stammer that I had to call her something.

'I didn't have the nerve to write your real name.'

'I wouldn't have advised it,' she says in her emphatically grown-up, ironically schoolmarmish tone, which is enough to take me back 30 years, and draws her cheeks up further, showing her teeth: flawless. I'd expected her to have got rid of the gap in her teeth, the gap I had wished I could disappear through 30 years ago.

Without having greeted her properly I ask, not just out of courtesy to the people queuing up, if she has time later; I notice that I have to collect myself, I have to find the words again that I'd prepared down to the last phrase for our encounter. She nods and immediately moves out of my field of view, waits in the foyer or maybe just a step behind me. While I write my name in the books of strangers, I compare the woman who doesn't want to be called Jutta over and over again with the girl I had once looked at adoringly in the smokers' corner.

Certainly I feared her anger, as I had made her a character in a novel without asking, and was prepared for her to throw my memories back in my face as mere fantasies. But that wasn't the only reason, not even the main reason for the trepidation I felt when I thought of the meeting I had so longed for. It was time that I feared more than anything else. Nowadays, when I meet friends after decades, I brace myself mechanically for the melancholy of seeing my own transience mirrored in their faces. To pre-empt my disappointment, I imagined even the schoolyard beauty with every shade of aging, now thickset and wrinkly with cracked lips, the corners of her mouth slumped downwards and cheeks like crumpled laundry on the clothesline, dressed badly to boot, and not half as clever as she seemed to the 15-year-old me, a careworn woman of mature years who has nothing in common with the fun-loving high school graduate except her name, or at most, some characteristic feature like a slightly upturned nose. As a reader of Proust, when I sit down at the table for the signing session, I almost ritually recall the matinee at the end of *In Search of Lost Time*, where the novelist returns to the world of the Guermantes decades later, and initially fails to recognize any of his acquaintances because they all seem to have put on masks, like at a costume ball, mostly by heavily powdering their faces, which completely changes them. The men still make the familiar faces, gestures, quips, but seem to have donned white beards, put lead soles on their feet and adorned their faces with wrinkles and shaggy eyebrows. And then the women: entire epochs must have rolled past for such revolutions to take place in the geology of their faces, whether erosions along a nose or an accretion on the shores of their cheeks, its opaque masses erupting into their faces with countless ruptures. 'I was told a name and I was stunned by the thought that it applied both to the fair-haired woman I remembered waltzing long ago and the large lady with white hair ponderously crossing the room near me.'

It costs enormous effort to gaze at an old comrade or an early love with both one's eyes and one's memory, and no one is more familiar with this effort than a novelist, or any other roving artist who is accosted time and again by a stranger claiming to be a friend. The stranger doesn't consider the fact that they are getting ready for the encounter as soon as they buy their ticket, that they know a recent photo from the posters and have imperceptibly familiarized themselves with the lines that have been drawn on the novelist's face, the hairs that have been plucked from his head, the padding that has been fastened to his belly. What I go through during the seconds or sometimes even full minutes that it takes to recognize someone, on the other hand, is always the matinee that Proust describes so unforgettably towards the end of *Lost Time*:

And now it dawned on me what old age was—old age, which of all realities, is perhaps the one we continue longest to think of in purely abstract terms, looking at calendars, dating our letters, seeing our friends marry, and then our friends' children, without understanding, whether out of fear or laziness, what it all means, until the day when we see a silhouette we do not recognize, like that of M. d'Argencourt, which makes us realise that we are living in a new world; until the day when the grandson of one of our friends, a young man whom we instinctively treat as an equal, smiles as if we were making fun of him, as to him we have always seemed like a grandfather; now I understood the meaning of death, loves, the pleasures of the mind, the use of suffering, a vocation, etc. For while names had lost their individuality for me, words were yielding up their full meaning. The beauty of images lies behind things, the beauty of ideas in front of them. So that the former cease to impress us when we reach them, whereas we have to go beyond the latter in order to understand them.

How surprised I am to find Jutta still just as attractive 30 years later, though in a different way: dainty now, even the curve of her belly is delicate, her shoulders so narrow that I want to take hold of her not just out of excitement, but almost a protective instinct of sorts, more friendship than infatuation; and how relieved I am to hear that cheerful, recognisably affectionate irony in her voice. Was Proust wrong? Even though I know it's just a pipe dream, I can't help hoping that she's just as lonely as I am, let's say, divorced, maybe children or maybe not, and that our schoolyard romance might yet turn out to be divine providence. In my mind I sketch the rest of the evening we'll spend together, the night at her flat or in my hotel room, imagine waking up in her arms, and after breakfast, taking a stroll through the small town where she's ended up, already wording the phone calls and letters with which we'll stay in contact, I imagine our reunion and the love that won't spring up in a second any more, but will last forever.

Time and again I resolve to concentrate on the people holding out the novel to me, the one I read from tonight, and get into brief conversations to bring my thoughts, which are going wild, under control again. After signing the last book I'm already filled with the worry that after 30 years, I'm still the boy who screws up love like an exam; I half wish that she's long since gone home, leaving me to hold onto the memory of our meeting as a sweet dream. But after looking around for her in vain, I jump from the stage to hurry into the foyer. It'll only occur to my editor afterwards that what happens to me with Jutta is the same as the novelist's experience with Odette in *Lost Time*: 'One starts with the idea that people have remained the same and one discovers that they have grown old. But if one starts by thinking them old, one does not find them so bad.'

The Head of Cultural Affairs stops me in the foyer and asks me to sort out the contractual business quickly before we go to dinner, and then a third and a fourth person join us, assaulting me with questions that I answer conscientiously while my eyes scan the crowd, who are refreshing themselves with pretzels and wine. Nor do I see Jutta at the book table, the first place I'd expect her to be. I excuse myself, saying I have to check on an old friend, she's waiting outside the door, I'll be back in a minute.

'Your friend is welcome to join us for dinner,' the Head of Cultural Affairs, who is also responsible for tourism, calls after me.

Naturally what I'd like to do is link arms with Jutta and go for a walk, but I don't want to offend my hosts, who found more listeners for me, and more attentive ones, than I could really expect in a small town like this. I'd have to come up with an excuse like a migraine or backache, and it would still sadden them. Besides that, another reason to take her along to the restaurant occurs to me: it might help me get over my trepidation if I spoke to Jutta in a larger group first. When I discover her on the pavement outside the multi-purpose hall, I look at her more closely than I did the first time. I quickly realize that I wouldn't have the courage anyway to take her hand uninvited and march off with her. With Odette too, the novelist has armed himself with far more than just a negative expectation, I'll insist to my editor, who finds fault with everything: her appearance seems to defy the rules of temporality, 'a more miraculous defiance of the laws of chronology than the conservation of radium was of the laws of nature'. Luckily, Jutta is also in conversation with some people, older than us, so presumably her husband or lover isn't among them, so I just call out the invitation to come and eat with us; the organisers have reserved a table and I can't really avoid the obligatory socializing. Jutta agrees with a nod, as if she hadn't expected anything else.

While I push my way back to the Head of Cultural Affairs with my head down to avoid being spoken to, I wonder whether the idea that Jutta has of me isn't as much a product of her imagination as my 30-year longing for her. For as unreal as it seems to me each time, and as vain as it is to mention it, one aspect of the circumstances in which we've met again is that I have a certain standing, arriving in a small town as a well-travelled author whose books are reviewed in national papers and even held up on TV. It's not just the celebrity—any weather woman on a regional channel is better known and more widely admired than a member of the literary scene. It's more that we evoke a romantic notion of the writer, if at all, for the audience in a provincial town, which is not particularly large, mostly female and older, and along with the writer the cliche of the anti-bourgeois globe-trotter, and sometimes, if the ladies have been staring for too long at the posters on which we always look so serious, even the far-sighted thinker and profound melancholic. And then, on stage, it seems that I sometimes radiate a confidence—or, far more surprisingly, a cheerfulness, supposedly even wisdom, that no one who met me in private would ever associate with me. That exerts a certain attraction, I like to think, especially for women who may have dreamt of a different life once—so for Jutta too?

I will only realize that I am the one falling for a cliche, not her, when I write the novel the reader is holding: the provincial woman whose life seemingly plods along uneventfully within clear boundaries, next to a busy husband and two perfectly brought-up children, while her heart trembles with unfulfilled, agonizing longing for something she doesn't know, because she feels that she is growing old, old without getting anything out of life except the boring, steady treadmill with the same motions, encounters and duties. 'She always thought of Paris,' as Guy de Maupassant put it. The scenario is practically a staple of French literature: the big city writer and the wife of some notary in the provinces. For Jutta I'm Paris, so to speak!, I think to myself, adding a soft layer of plush to reality while the Head of Cultural Affairs enters the travel expenses in the contract form. 'She was still pretty. The uneventful life she lived had preserved her like a winter apple in an attic. Yet she was consumed from within by unspoken and obsessive desires. She wondered if she would die without ever having tasted the wicked delights which life had to offer, without ever, not even once, having plunged into the ocean of voluptuous pleasure which, to her, was Paris.'

The reader who may have felt that the Proust quotes were reasonably suitable will perhaps find it odd to see Maupassant mentioned as well. Yes, let me respond immediately to the question that I would also put to myself as a reader, yes, there is a plan behind it: the French literature of the nineteenth and early twentieth century runs through the novel the reader is holding; the following pages will hopefully show how and why more conclusively than any number of explanations could. And no, to answer the next question I would ask if I were reading the novel I will write (a bouquet for the editor so that he'll let that monster of a sentence pass)—no, of course I don't mentally recite Proust or even think of Maupassant's name while running agitatedly back and forth between Jutta and the Head of Cultural Affairs. Even as the novelist I just happen to be, I don't carry more than a shadow of literary history around with me as I go through life. And what I'm thinking now, as I put the unopened envelope with the reading fee in the inside pocket of my jacket, is far less orderly, considered or informed than the stream of ideas in the novel I will write. After all, I'm not walking about with a Dictaphone or a digital pocket library. And because the immediacy imposed linguistically by the present tense is just as constructed, just as much an inevitable consequence of gaining awareness as any other literary form, I can sprinkle in a few quotations that not even the best reader would think of spontaneously.

On the short walk to the restaurant through the small town, which seems deserted but is probably just sleeping by quarter to ten at night, I learn that Jutta studied medicine and then worked on the continent of her favourite reading, as she calls Latin America, with the same gentle, almost smug irony that she generally seems to apply to our past. There she fell in love with her later husband—no, not a guérillero, she anticipates my next question, but a German who was her colleague, they got married at the registry office in Quito with . . .

'Just imagine!' Jutta sighs nostalgically.

. . . brightly-dressed Indigenous families in the hallway who congratulated them, singing and clapping, when they stepped out of the room.

I just say, 'Wow'.

When they were expecting their second child, the couple moved back to Germany, first working at a hospital until his parents found the practice, which was big enough for both of them and affordable as well. Sure, they would have preferred to stay in the city, but they hadn't accumulated any capital during their time abroad; just thinking about the future had gone against their ideology. Now there are three children, 21, 16 and 14 years old, so starting again somewhere new is out of the question, says Jutta, although she still longs to travel.

'And once the children are out of the house?' I ask.

'I don't think I'll manage to get my husband away from here now,' says Jutta, without sounding at all sorrowful.

Maybe she just wants to set out her position as a happily married woman. Or she knows how Maupassant's story ends: the big city writer whom the provincial woman had imagined to be wild and passionate went to sleep prematurely!

> The night hours passed silently save for the ticking of the clock as, motionless, she thought of her conjugal nights at home.
>
> By the yellow light of a Chinese lantern, she looked in dismay at the tubby little man beside her, lying on his back with the sheet draped over his hot-air balloon of a body.
>
> While he snored like a pipe organ, with comic interludes of lengthy, strangulated snorts, the few hairs he possessed, exhausted by the onerous responsibility of masking the ravages of time on his balding skull during the day, now stood perkily on end. A dribble of saliva flowed from the corner of his half-open mouth.

To my amazement, I don't have to introduce Jutta to anyone at the table, and the others ask her, not me, how we know each other. Spontaneously or not, she lies that we met during her time in Latin America. As glad as I am to keep our secret safe, I still check whether she gave a little wink in my direction; as soon as we're alone, I certainly want to ask her about our schoolyard romance. Except Jutta doesn't look at me during the whole of dinner, even though I'm sitting next to her. She leads the conversation as if she were tonight's guest, and, after two comments on the reading that are more dutiful than courteous, she and the others focus on local matters: the sensor-controlled traffic lights, which work wonders at the slip road to the motorway, the cancellation of lessons at the primarily school, the second grass pitch for the football club. I realize with consternation that the reading evidently didn't make as profound an impression as I'd thought on stage; no one even notices that Jutta has the turned-up nose highlighted in the novel.

After readings I always hope I won't have to answer any questions, but each time I'm disappointed if no one's interested in my book any more. On this occasion my presence is even bothersome, as I'm blocking the people on my right's view of Jutta, who is increasingly dominating the conversation; when I lean forwards to eat, the man directly next to me is even brazen enough to prop himself up on my chair behind my back for a better look. Keeping my eyes on my schnitzel, I prepare myself inwardly for the fiasco that the evening is heading for. I was ready for anything—just not for a re-run of the old schoolyard scenario, with her surrounded by friends while I languish on the sidelines, after only half an hour. Because the more often I sneak a glance at her, the more beautiful she seems, incredibly self-assured, giving full attention to everyone who speaks to her, and with enviable fervour, even if it's only about traffic light control.

I don't know how many pointers I've already missed by the time I finally realize that Jutta is the mayor of this small town.

Afterwards I learn that unlike most people who wanted to prevent nuclear armament 30 years ago, she never gave up the struggle for a better world; she chose to study medicine because it promised a direct alleviation of suffering, and in Latin America she put her political views into practice. Back in Germany, the children and later the new practice didn't leave much time for other things, but she could at least take on local problems. It was through her involvement with the day care centre and yes, the introduction of separate rubbish bins, that she got into local politics and brought herself to join a party, so that she could actually make changes happen instead of just demanding them. She was something of a poster girl, she herself says, as a young working woman who was active in the church and—as I add myself, before immediately feeling embarrassed about the lousy compliment—practically made for election ads, and was soon nominated for the local council. While her work as a doctor in Latin America had been fulfilling, she found the general practice she shared with her husband less and less satisfying: rushing through six patients an hour because the health insurance companies forced them to, then the weekends spent doing the accounts and finally her own cynicism, which started to creep in because most patients had little aches and pains compared to the unfortunates she had treated in Latin America. There she had saved lives, but here she often just helped bored pensioners pass their time. She already got laws on afternoon childcare and waste separation passed during her first term in office.

We've got to the spirits now, and the conversation is still stuck in local politics; everyone at the table thinks Jutta has good chances in the next election, which has been the topic of discussion since dessert. I make an effort not to sound patronizing, and tell myself that my world seems just as small from the outside; after all, writers just talk about their own affairs at dinner too—sales figures, reading fees, reviews—which are even more insignificant to outsiders. But it continues to nag at me that the reading I considered a success barely an hour earlier is now appearing in a much paler light. That no one seems to notice Jutta's upturned nose, the colour of her hair and, above all, her smile, and that no one is adding together 19 and 30 years—hardly testifies to a lasting memory of my novel. It's nothing new for me, especially in small towns like these, which often don't even have a bookshop: I get a slot between the women's choir and the touring theatre so that they'll have a bit of literature in their annual record. And with someone like me, the culture office can tick the integration box at the same time.

Just when my gloom has gained such a hold on me that it promises to engulf the whole night in my obligatory single room, I feel Jutta's hand on my wrist under the table. Has she noticed how lost I feel in this group? It's not really a caress; her fingers don't move, and it seems more like a calming gesture, and yet there is ultimately something conspiratorial about it. Wait, her hand seems to be saying, wait until we're out of here, then we'll talk properly. I look at Jutta, but she's just promising a tough election campaign.

On the stroll we take through town, because there's nowhere to go for a drink, we pass the two grass pitches: one lengthwise with a narrow seating area, the other one new, so presumably for training. The football team has been promoted to the third division, Jutta tells me, and says it's amazing because all the other teams in the division come from towns with populations of thirty or forty thousand.

'Is that already professional?' I ask, to keep the conversation going.

'No, not professional,' Jutta replies, 'but it felt like the German Championship.'

It's not that Jutta's élan leaves me cold, or that I'm ignoring her achievements in life: her courage and her willingness to make sacrifices in going to Latin America instead of pursuing a career, and then starting again in Germany, setting up a medical practice and bringing up three children, no doubt great guys, her success as a young politician in a small town that had always been governed by older men. As a novelist, I would be the first to affirm that one can make any place the centre of the world. And Jutta looks stunning too—her eyes, sparkling warmly with the light of the street lamps, her idiosyncratic nose, her lithe body, restless with excess energy. I just feel that I can't connect to her. We walk so closely together that our shoulders keep touching, we act like friends who haven't seen each other for too long, we talk about our lives as if it went without saying that it's of interest. But what really connects us—that one week when we ate ice cream in front of the train station every afternoon and spent three nights together—she doesn't go anywhere near that or say a word about the novel I read from tonight.

'It probably doesn't seem important to someone like you,' Jutta says once she no longer expects a response from me, 'but the business with the football pitch was really a big deal for me.'

'Tell me about the football pitch,' I reply so quickly that I'm not sure myself if my request is just an attempt to hide my disinterest.

As a roving artist, which I simply happen to be as a novelist, I often deal with the mayors of unassuming communities and smaller towns. I've been invited to present my book or give the celebratory speech at a New Year's reception; the officials have already gone home, even the lobby is empty, and then the mayor invites me into his office. I'm curious; I keep asking things, to the mayor's delight, and he suggests a little tour. That'd be very nice, I reply courteously, whereupon the mayor picks up the phone and tells someone—his wife or the outside office, where someone is still waiting to call it a day—that he'll be gone for half an hour or maybe delayed for an hour. A moment later I'm standing beside a man who may be no older than me, there are so many younger mayors nowadays, after all; but with his tie and side parting, he simply looks different, he took a different path than I did (although I was born in a small town too), he didn't protest against nuclear armament or fight for the revolution in Latin America, he joined the student council at school instead, didn't go to university, or he did and moved back to the provinces afterwards—we're standing in the courtyard, grey in grey, and the mayor tells me how it was renovated at great expense, but that it was so necessary, speaking with as much passion as if it were St Peter's Basilica. And the trees, lawn and fountain that the mayor conjures up before my inner eye are just the beginning: as we walk around and he talks about the bigger tasks, accomplished and unaccomplished—the young people who can't find trainee positions, the Turks who shouldn't be praying in a garage any more, the noise from the thoroughfare depriving residents of sleep and so on and so forth—the tasks never end—I think as I keep asking one question after another, to his great joy, I think: Yes, you're right, it's not always about me, what you're doing here is important, not what I do; and I feel like grabbing the mayor by his upper arms and shaking, and calling out to him, the way no one ever grabs me after a reading: You did well to stay in this small town.

Later I'll be unable to recall what exactly Jutta says about the second football pitch, something about people from different backgrounds getting along, the asylum seekers' hostel and a Nigerian who contributed to the championships—but here my feeling that someone is in the right place, solving problems as concrete as a loaf of bread or a sip of milk, and an admiration commanded by something as simple as a healthy, fair-trade school breakfast, is stronger than in other small towns, because she doesn't belong here. She simply made some place, a completely arbitrary place where she happened to be, the centre of the world. With some trees, a lawn and a fountain, even the courtyard of the town hall wouldn't be grey any more.

I wonder whether Jutta is refraining from asking about my divorce, which is mentioned several times in the novel I read from tonight, out of the same inhibition that makes me avoid the subject of her marriage. Probably it's much simpler and she's just not interested in my private life—and why would she be? Our past love affair goes equally unmentioned, and then we've already gone round the whole town and explained the government's infrastructure law too. But I must say, for all the disappointment, the conversation is stimulating nonetheless; I learn a few things about everyday German life and find myself seeing other things in a new, even a more favourable light, though admittedly I'd be more open to that if I weren't constantly thinking about what's in Jutta's head, let alone her heart, wondering what questions and experiences preoccupy her outside of her work—not just her marriage, but what she thinks about life and her life in general, whether she's burdened by troubles she would never share with a stranger like me, and whether the thanks we get for our existence is really an experience or at best an acknowledgement.

'I just don't want to stop talking to you,' I blurt out in the middle of her sentence, surprising myself with the intimacy my own words seek to create.

Jutta stops and turns to me, her cheeks like apricots again. I find myself thinking that consciously or unconsciously, she'll use that smile, which seems so disarmingly caring, in her next election campaign.

'Let's have a glass of wine at my place,' she suggests, and after I fail to react immediately—could it be that she senses I was caught off guard, or does she want to rule out any misunderstanding?—adds that then I could meet her husband too, as he never goes to bed before two o'clock.

'Doesn't he have to get up very early?' I ask, even though it's the last thing that's on my mind. 'As a doctor, I mean.'

'Oh sure,' Jutta answers, and explains that her husband could even get by on four hours' sleep when they lived in Ecuador. 'Or don't you drink?'

'I've been doing it all evening.'

'Oh right, so you have.'

When I write this novel, I'll change just enough details along with the name that no one will recognize the woman I loved in the schoolyard. So maybe she's not a mayor at all, or doesn't have a bob hairstyle, maybe not even an upturned nose or blonde hair, which would mean that the trickery already started in the novel I read from tonight. For the novel the reader is holding I will alter more still, even substantially if I see fit, taking on board painful omissions if necessary so that Jutta, who is not called Jutta, will agree to its publication. But I'll document the feeling that seeing her again gives me, the many conflicting feelings, as precisely as possible. In general, as a novelist, I only actually invent things where it serves—I like the phrase, which I know from crime films—to find the truth. After all, I wouldn't even claim to know my own truth, to know what I'm feeling right now, how I see the world and so on. Differently put: I know what I feel, see and so on, or think I know, but the meaning of some experience or other often becomes more opaque the more meaningful it seems. That's the only reason I write, and I only do so where I don't understand something I saw, heard or felt, whether in the big or the small things. And I'll have to report on that renewed meeting after a reading—and that part is true, in the conventional sense—being together unrecognized at the restaurant, the walk through an unknown, seemingly deserted small town that I'd normally forget the next morning, the invitation to the detached house she shares with her husband and three children, and everything I learn in one night about love—precisely because it will glow more and more darkly with meaning.

As a precaution, let me say to any reader expecting some kind of drama after this interjection, maybe even a criminal case after my reference to 'finding the truth', to this reader who is of course welcome, but maybe not so suitable for the novels I write, that the night won't offer anything spectacular, no bedroom scene, not even a kiss. It will be nothing and yet so much, and it is precisely in this gap between a meaninglessness that becomes apparent even to the lovers themselves and an overwhelming sense of significance even to outsiders—those with an empathetic view, that is—in this tiny space that I have overlooked or considered insignificant until now, until walking through the town and entering her house, that there may be some heaven promised to humans by God. Yes, it will be the exact opposite of the novel I read from tonight: the recounted events will seem trivial to the lovers themselves, and yet they will be everything that love on earth promises.

Although I should have expected it (he's a doctor, she's a mayor), I'm surprised by the size of the—well, it's a real villa, a venerable old building with three floors, with windows upstairs that extend to the ground, evidently enlarged later, probably bedrooms behind them, a double garage as an annexe and solar panels on the roof.

'Are there some on the garage too?'

'Yes,' Jutta replies. 'We even supply electricity.'

'And it pays off?'

'It does now, yes.'

It's her husband, I learn, whose ecological awareness and foible for technical innovation are so great that, over the years, he's expanded the old building into a model of nature-friendly living: rain water use, thorough insulation, natural gas extraction and . . . I can't keep up with Jutta as she lists the facilities that reduce the consumption of natural resources or even produce resources. By now we're already standing in the hallway, where the children don't have to be quite so tidy: shoes of different sizes strewn across the floor, bicycle helmets, a skateboard and a basketball that has rolled against the black leather doctor's bag, bright yellow rainwear haphazardly tossed on the dresser, and in between all that, some detachable bicycle lamps and a pile of DVDs of Hollywood films.

'Making the big windows smaller, that's something I managed to prevent,' whispers Jutta. 'And the two cars are totally indispensable for us.'

'But at least they're electric, right?' I ask, adopting not only the volume but also the tone in which she speaks about her husband's foible.

'He has to make do with hybrid,' Jutta replies. 'He wouldn't get far with an electric out here in the country.'

'What about you?'

'I like my official car best,' Jutta chuckles.

'Shall I take my shoes off?'

'Yes, please.'

The first time, because I'm untying my own shoelaces, I only catch it from the corner of my eye; but the second time, I see the movement in all its graceful glory, the way she now draws her left calf towards her bottom while both turning and bending her upper body as nimbly as a dancer, the way she holds the heel and lifts her foot out of the equally elegant shoe and then, truly a dancer now, so light, the way she throws her calf forwards to send the shoe flying off her foot to land in between the children's sneakers. Is it really her? I ask myself; Jutta, who wasn't called Jutta, wasn't as short or slender as the woman in front of me, who walks inside the house in nylon stockings as naturally as if I were a family member or a daily guest. That's right: when she took me home with her 30 years ago, she also went ahead and went straight from the door through the hallway and up the stairs to her room, without looking back—except back then I didn't notice, or I can't remember, whether she moved with the same confidence; my memory hasn't preserved any gesture with a comparable elegance to those tossed-off shoes. But now I record every glance and every motion, her lightly spread fingers as she walks, her bottom, rocking back and forth in the tight skirt, this striking—yes, that's the strongest impression—this striking automatism in the way she moves, which negates the obviously unfamiliar, unrehearsed and unforeseeable nature of our situation.

'Hello, darling?' I hear her ask in the room, presumably the living room, that she has dancingly entered.

Even well-read people nowadays are often unaware that the most famous statement in *Minima Moralia*, that wrong life cannot be lived rightly, refers to modern furnishing. It seems that Jutta and her husband leave the decision about how one should live, in the concrete sense of dwelling—a problem that was already unsolvable 70 years ago—to their children. Presumably they chose the actual furniture, but the light brown leather couch set, the pine shelves with the CD rack next to it, the dark blue reading chair with a footrest and movable backrest, and finally the light-coloured rug made of new wool on the stone floor, are spread very sparsely across the large living room, which was built back in the days of evening salons. But what strikes me most is that the furniture looks as if it's been chosen at random from one of the tacky brochures I sometimes find in my letterbox. There's not one piece that I haven't seen looking exactly the same in a hundred other living rooms or in adverts; if anything, I'm surprised that the ordinariness of the furnishing doesn't quite suit the two medical professions, or rather one and the mayoral position, let alone the stateliness of a street in which the trees and villas are older than the oldest people.

But then, it seems to me that the furnishing isn't important, that Jutta and her husband don't consider it important; it's simply the fixed decor of a stage on which the performances change as the children grow up. The stains on the sofa support the argument that it would not be worth investing a great deal in the furniture. Aside from the unexpectedly large bookshelf, which I will examine more closely, individuality is expressed only by the children: the schoolbooks and homework diaries on the coffee table, the unfinished board game on the floor, the clothes dropped at random, as well as a used cereal bowl that no one cleared away, glasses, some of them still half-full, a bag of crisps with half its contents scattered on the couch, DVDs of American romances and comedies in front of the TV cabinet, two more bags of crisps and a hairbrush, an electric guitar leaning against an amplifier; at least there are some headphones on top of the amp in case the feedback bothers anyone.

I remember that I neglected to ask anything much about the children when Jutta mentioned them; now I've already forgotten how old they are and whether they're boys or girls. Going by the football jersey that's also lying on the floor, she must have a son, I'd guess around 12 or 13, as well as a daughter, if I've assigned the hairbrush between the DVDs correctly, and then a second son who plays the electric guitar. Or does the guitar belong to the crisp-eating girl, and the eldest child—whether son or daughter—is already out of the house? In the corner is a barbell, two mighty weights attached to a glinting bar that probably isn't lifted by Jutta. Maybe it belongs to her husband, who presumably agreed to convert the bourgeois living room into a hobby space or suggested it himself. In the end that's exactly what we wanted when we rebelled against our elders—Jutta more fiercely, in the squat—except that we didn't depose our parents but ourselves, as we're the elders now. Where has she got to?

When Jutta enters the living room, she's no longer the same person. She's wearing the same dress, the same nylon stockings without shoes, the same tasteful make-up as ten minutes ago, no traces of tear-smudged eye shadow; but her look, her mischievous, clearly affectionate and at once slightly patronizing, and thus ironically inflected gaze, has vanished. Gone is the feather-light, seemingly innate determination that has enchanted me since we met again; what I see is a woman who seems as helpless as someone abandoned, and somehow older as a result, strangely, although helplessness and certainly lovesickness often give a face a certain childlike quality. Lovesickness? My spontaneous association of her sadness with lovesickness probably has more to do with my memories than her appearance; it's more accurate to say that there is something deadly tired, or even already dead about her face. I can see that she's weighing up, her mouth already open, whether to try glossing over her distress or just tell me right now what happened; whether I of all people, practically a stranger, would be someone she could open up to, or she should politely see me out. I finally notice how much effort it's taking for her to unfreeze.

'Shall I go, or do you want me to stay?'

'No, stay,' says Jutta, surprising me with the speed of her answer. 'Doesn't have to be for long.'

My assumption that she's argued with her husband at least turns out to be partly true.

'We don't even argue any more,' Jutta explains.

She knocked on the door of the study, where he was still doing the accounts, planted a kiss next to his lips and told him that she'd brought the school friend who read tonight at the community centre. Her husband knows about the book, so he also knows about the love I felt for his wife, though she didn't feel as strongly about me. He had been planning to accompany her to the reading, but his consultations dragged on again. He's not touchy or jealous towards me—why would he be?—on the contrary, he was curious to meet me and had said that morning that he'd come along to dinner after the reading. Funnily enough, both he and Jutta had expected to find me likeable.

'And you are,' Jutta assures me, not realizing that there is nothing a man in love wants to hear less than praise for his niceness, however far in the past his desire might be.

All evening I've resented the totally untroubled way she looks at me, speaks to me and touches my arm; and the fact that her husband was even looking forward to meeting me is further evidence that they don't take my passion particularly seriously.

'But something must've happened for you to be so done in,' I say.

Her husband had already got up to follow her into the living room when he asked her, as if in passing, to make the children some food the next time they were both out; after all, chocolate muesli is hardly a suitable meal for a 14 year old who's been playing football all afternoon, and crisps are all very well, but he doesn't see why there had to be three half-eaten packs lying around in the living room. And the couch was filthy again. All she needed to do was smile at him or sigh and put her arms around his neck, and her husband would be sitting on the couch next to me now; she could have said all sorts of things, could have justified herself or countered with some accusation of her own—Why didn't *you* clear away the crisps?—and the discord would already have dissipated on the stairs. But too often, she stood before him with the feeling that he was attacking her where she was most vulnerable on purpose, out of malice, by mocking her in a deliberately casual way about her carelessness with the children. And then she doesn't just want to justify herself or throw the accusation back at him, she'd love to just scream at him in that moment, just throw things at him. She doesn't, of course, and didn't do it this time either. She just turned around, closed the door of the study behind her and knew very well that her silent exit would establish the disharmony between them— leaving him standing there without comment, while downstairs the old school friend with whom she once had a relationship, however short, however long ago, is waiting. It will take days for them to exchange more than the bare necessities, and weeks, if not months, for them to embrace again.

'And all that over three bags of crisps?' I ask.

'Sometimes we even manage for no reason at all.'

'Maybe it's a particular sign of love,' I try to comfort her, 'that you take even the smallest things so seriously.'

'What is that anyway—love?'

I declared or asserted earlier that I only write because, or when, I don't understand something. The reader, especially the professional reader, seems to imagine the exact opposite; since the publication of the novel I read from tonight, I am regularly asked about love and, believe it or not, invited to speak as an expert on TV and the radio. Not that I go along with any old nonsense; but if someone asks me my opinion after a reading or in a letter, maybe even requests some advice, I can't just shrug my shoulders. So I say or write down whatever seems most plausible, or something I've already prepared for similar questions, and at least try to come across as likeable in case my reply isn't enough. And at times, I think I don't sound all that foolish. It verges on charlatanry, I admit. If someone took the various pieces of advice I've given here and there and put them next to one another, they wouldn't think they had all come from one and the same person. It's literature, if anything, that establishes the congruence which experience doesn't offer. I can't speak here for all novelists; no doubt there are wiser and more knowledgeable ones than me, especially when it comes to love. But precisely in matters of love, my life shows clearly enough that I haven't understood anything. I don't have to go into detail about my divorce, though maybe I'd note that my son, who is looked after alternately by his mother and me, has slipped away from me entirely now; we hardly talk any more, even though there's no creature in the world I love more. So as far as love is concerned, all I have to show are ruins. And now I'm sitting in the living room of the woman who, 30 years ago, I didn't just adore, but truly worshipped more passionately than anyone has worshipped a god, I'm sitting opposite her on a couch at 20 to 12 in an unfamiliar small town, the everyday items of her almost grown-up children scattered all around, and she asks me in all seriousness what love is.

If I carried a digital pocket library around with me, I could share the insights of knowledgeable and even wise novelists with Jutta that always elude my memory when I need them. On the other hand, it would be a little cringeworthy to palm her off with literary snippets in her need, and the novel I will write quotes often enough from Proust, who—even Proust!—remarks with a sigh that 'in all matters concerning love, it is better if one does not even try to understand anything.' In search of something to say, without giving an answer that would be no more or less true than its opposite, I return to Jutta's past, of which I still have to provide some cursory description for the reader, and ask what made her go to Latin America as a young woman.

'I mean, that was pretty unusual, wasn't it?'

'Well, we all had Nicaragua on our radar at the time.'

Yet it wasn't in the revolutionary San Salvador, but at the clinic of an internationally renowned doctor in Quito that she found a position which would be recognized in Germany as an elective for her degree. Soon she heard about the young German man who was treating Indigenous patients—not alone, but as the partner of a local doctor who flew from village to village in little propeller planes. She got his number and called to ask if she could accompany him for a week; she felt out of place at the clinic, which could just as easily have been in Germany, while he promised the kind of life that had made her want to study medicine. By the time she flew back to Quito they were a couple, and she already felt strongly that they could remain one for a lifetime. He, on the other hand, would later admit that he was initially just happy to have unexpectedly found someone who occasionally shared his bed, his thoughts and simply his language. That asynchronicity in the onset of love in their relationship already contained the seed of the reproaches, injuries and withdrawals that now raise the question of whether the love hasn't long since left their relationship.

'But it could be the other way around,' I counter.

'How do you mean?'

'That the reproaches, injuries and withdrawals, as you put it, simply act as justifications for the fact that you don't love each other any more.'

'But I didn't say that we don't love each other any more.'

My objection didn't make me more likeable, I realize, while Jutta stares silently at the bowl in which the remains of the chocolate muesli are drying out.

'I just asked you what love is anyway,' she says after a few seconds, in a way that makes it sound like an accusation.

'If only I knew!' I reply apologetically.

He was still new in the team himself, the very first foreigner in the area; he'd wanted to share the bread of the local helpers, not represent the Western aid industry. Of course he was naive, says Jutta, so young after all, early thirties, carried by the wish to help and happy to do so every day. Looking back today, she understands why he accepted her passion rather than sharing it; he was consumed by his work, confronted with a misery that was literally naked, he saved lives or had to announce deaths, often enough caused by the circumstances—poverty, lack of medication, lack of equipment, imported pathogens. The relatives would already be standing by the short strip of meadow that had been cleared in the jungle as a runway, waiting to take him to the patients. The gratitude they showed him—and her, even though she was just a guest, his apprentice—wiped the stress and strain from their faces like sweat. Then, says Jutta, while the propeller plane took off to go to the next village, he smiled, he smiled at her too, as if he had received the greatest gift. Clearly, then, there was no space there for love, for an egotistical love of his own. From today's perspective, she loved him for the very thing she would reproach him for.

'Sounds a bit like *The English Patient*,' I say, trying to make the respect in my words audible.

'You mean *Rules of the Wild*,' she corrects in the motherly, or rather big-sisterly tone she already adopted when she greeted me.

I think I mean some other film.

Jutta goes to the terrace for a smoke.

'Take a pair,' she says, pointing to the plastic slippers piled up behind the glass door.

I haven't mentioned yet that it's late February; winter is hopefully over, but it's still too cold to stay outside for long without a jacket, so I take the fleece blanket outside that's lying in front of the TV and put it around her shoulders.

'Thank you,' she says, and lifts up one end of the blanket so I can stand next to her.

Now we're really our young selves again, I think, cuddling up and shivering in a garden that could belong to our parents, whether hers or mine. If cigarettes didn't give me headaches, I'd light one up too. It's enough having the smoke blowing in my direction.

'Hey, you're smoking pot,' I remark, only recognizing the smell at the second drag.

'You want some?' Jutta asks, holding out the joint.

'I don't smoke,' I reply, but accept her offer anyway. I swiftly start coughing.

'I can tell.'

'What?'

'That you don't smoke.'

She at least seems less obviously distressed than when she entered the living room: she already lectured me, now she's teasing me.

'Isn't that dangerous?' I ask.

'Nicotine or alcohol are more dangerous, any doctor'll tell you that.'

'No, I mean for you as the mayor.'

'Oh, that's what you mean.'

'If someone sees you with a joint.'

'No one'll see me at home,' Jutta says, taking the joint back. 'And, as a matter of fact, I'm lobbying at the national level for a legalization of cannabis.'

'Oh, so that's how you come up with your manifesto?'

'If you'd ended up in a backwater like this, you'd treat yourself to an evening puff too.'

Then she laughs exactly the same laugh described in the novel I read from tonight, with that transition from a smile where she draws her lips outwards, as if in slow motion, until her mouth finally has to open. There are a few more lines now, sure, which deepen into dimples as she laughs, and sadly the gap in her teeth has gone.

Looking at it again from today's perspective, her love was based more on the ideal she had formed in her mind, even before the first meeting, than on her husband himself. Of course, it wasn't something as simplistic as imagining Robert Redford saving seals after going to the cinema, but no doubt certain books and films became sedimented in her subconscious, and like many of our generation, she was inspired by the idea of offering something useful and yes, making the world a better place, however corny and maybe presumptuous that sounds today; but most of all, she wanted to get out of Germany, which was an unbearable place in itself. Germany was well fed and narrow-minded, and had become nationalistic again since the moral and intellectual shift.

'God yes, Kohl.'

'And it got even worse after reunification!' Jutta exclaims, and tells me why she applied to go to Latin America: 'Asylum seekers' hostels on fire everywhere, all that fascist shit coming back again.'

But in Latin America she was disappointed by the hospital in the capital, where the inequality seemed all the more ironclad cast; there was the question of what she could do with her studies or her life in general after coming back, how she could prevent it from going against her noble intentions, as well as the question of children, which was already on her mind—she was more ecologically motivated than a leftist as such, and choosing motherhood and a family didn't contradict her political aware-ness, which was actually quite old-fashioned, as she says . . .

'Christian too?' I interject.

'Yes, liberation theology and all that.'

. . . and suddenly, in the middle of the jungle, the most remote spot in the universe, she meets this young German doctor who had Indigenous children clinging to his legs as soon as he got off the propeller plane. That was quite a sight, especially as the doctor was far from bad-looking, not some guy with a beard and shoulder-length hair the way she'd imagined, his hair was more like—I sense what actor she's about to name and think: please, not him!—more like Robert Redford, and she thought: yes, she could love someone like that, yet she hardly knew anything about him.

'So was it really love at that point?' I ask.

'No,' Jutta replies, 'love probably means that the other person gradually replaces the picture one's fallen in love with.'

'Hang on, I didn't quite follow that.'

'Well, that over the years, the other, as a real person with their own reality, covers up the projection one initially made of them.'

'You mean the beloved spreads themselves out in that love, as it were, which already exists independently of them?'

'Well, obviously not completely independently.'

'And, did he?'

'What?'

'Spread himself out in your love?'

'Yes, he did,' says Jutta, but perhaps too slowly.

'Evidently it was an especially big projection too.'

'I probably didn't make it easy for him.'

'Probably not.'

'Come on, let's go back indoors.'

Did Jutta tell me all of that, the whole beginning of her love, in the short time that it takes to smoke a joint? If I simply count the number of letters it might even add up, but when I write the novel I'll shorten the conversation, and what we say between the words, I'll move sentences and short dialogues from here to there without compunction, put them wherever they fit better, will no doubt misremember some things and exaggerate others, clothe them in my own words, fill in the gaps in my memory—that's just my profession. A mere transcript wouldn't even interest Jutta, who will read the novel too. But is it a novel then? Aside from a few externals that I'll alter, as I said, the meeting isn't invented at all. I tell the story of it in the same way a painter portrays a face or a landscape; whether they paint it realistically or not, it embodies that face or that landscape as accurately as possible and is nonetheless considered art, whereas today a novel is considered a novel, or a feature film considered a feature film, because it deviates from reality; otherwise it would be a documentary or a journal. On the other hand: what does it really tell us if the first-person narrator of a novel, purporting to be one and the same person as the novelist, claims that he is not writing a novel but simply documenting real events?

Jutta has already slipped out of the fleece blanket while I linger for a moment on the terrace to savour her touch, however emphatically platonic it was. No doubt there's also the scent of her perfume, mingled with the cannabis, but the sensation in my upper arm, which she leaned against freely, is much stronger. I could have put my arm around her without her misunderstanding the intimacy in which we had found ourselves since she returned to the living room upset—it was a conscious, deliberate process that I could observe—after she had decided neither to hide her distress nor ask me to leave.

I can't say to what extent she put her trust in me, the person whose youth she remembers in at least vague outlines, whom she had observed for an hour or longer on stage at her community centre and with whom she had taken a walk around her town, or whether I just happened to be standing there, like a passer-by in the street when someone trips up. And yet just now, shivering side by side under the fleece blanket, we shared more, and I was probably closer to her, than during our entire romance. And my face was even turned away so that the smoke wouldn't get up my nose! As big as not only our words had been, but also our feelings, hers too, for there must have been something about that boy that made her invite him into her den of mattresses—they weren't shared feelings; I only paid attention to my own infatuation, my rapture, my desire, my jealousy, my despair. Even in physical union, she wasn't what counted. Now I could have put my arm around her and she would have felt at once, and I would have meant it that way, that I was doing it for her, not for the sake of my own desire, my own fulfilment. On the other hand, what does it really mean in love if someone thinks they are doing something purely for the other? That was what I thought too, back then.

Back in the living room—Jutta has already sat down while I stand in front of the bookshelf—she says that she came across a great saying, supposedly from the twelfth century. Perhaps she's trying to change the subject, to shift the conversation away from her own sensibilities, or maybe just showing me that she knows something about my field. Or is she finally going to mention the novel I read from tonight? It does actually contain sayings from the twelfth century, several in fact.

'And?' I therefore ask, with genuine interest.

' "Love is not a justified argument against love." '

The statement is from Stendhal's book *On Love*, she tells me, which her husband bought himself when he found it mentioned in a review of my novel. I recall the review well; it was by a critic whose opinion has considerable weight, and the publisher put the comparison with Stendhal on the cover of the paperback edition.

'Did you read it?'

'I only dipped into it, to be honest,' Jutta replies. 'I was a bit disappointed.'

Realizing that I wasn't prepared for such a harsh judgement, I wordlessly turn back towards the bookshelf. But it only feels more idiotic to hide the dismay in my face from her so obviously.

'What was it that disappointed you?' I ask, turning around again.

'It's not even a proper novel, it's presented in kind of a scientific way, like a textbook, kind of pseudotheoretical, and then it's just full of run-of-the-mill sayings.'

I know that some people found my novel overly essayistic, but it's certainly not pseudotheoretical, let alone a textbook, and what she calls run-of-the-mill sayings are proverbs of mystics from centuries ago that have been largely forgotten even in the Orient.

'And it's a purely male view of love,' she adds, twisting the knife further. 'Maybe that was why I couldn't get much out of it.'

The reader will long since have realized that Jutta is talking about Stendhal's treatise; but fool that I am, in my vanity and affection, I overlook the obvious and agree with Jutta that it's a purely male view of love, but I say as much in the novel.

'I mean, the book talks about love from the boy's perspective,' I say, actually starting to justify my own work.

'What boy?'

'Well, the boy in the book. And that's why his love fails, precisely because he can't empathize with the girl and always just sees himself. That's the whole point of the story.'

Oh God! I exclaim inwardly: if a critic could see me now, breaking my novel down to a single basic message.

'But I don't mean your novel,' she says, showing her smile again, which strikes me as rather patronizing.

'What?'

'I mean Stendhal. I mean, of course Stendhal is great, but this book of his, this treatise on love, I found it all a bit thin.'

'But it's a nice saying,' I interject quickly, to prevent her dwelling on my misunderstanding. 'But why from the twelfth century?'

'Stendhal quotes it from a medieval tract or something.'

'If the first-person narrator of a literary work claims that it's an authentic text rather than a literary work, that doesn't mean it's necessarily true.'

Even as I reel off these words like some memorized rule—which is enough an effort already—I feel annoyed that after making an ass of myself, I'm now boring her with a lecture. But I continue nonetheless:

'Associating marriage with love doesn't really fit into the twelfth century at all. And it's so subtle too—marriage is . . . how did the saying go again?'

'Never mind,' says Jutta, ending the discussion on literary history, and asks whether I'd like a tea too, she's had enough wine for today.

After we've agreed on lemongrass—better not to have any caffeine at this hour—Jutta disappears into the kitchen. I'm surprised by how she takes it for granted that I'll stay longer. But I haven't dared to ask what the thinks of the novel I read from tonight.

Evidently Jutta left Latin America behind in literary terms too, assuming it was ever actually the continent of her favourite reading, as the shelf only features the usual names, in alphabetical order: García Marquez, Neruda, Vargas Llosa. Evidently she— or her husband, or both?—is more fond of the French; the great novels of the nineteenth and early twentieth century all seem to be there, including the huge multivolume edition of Balzac's *Human Comedy*. So that's why her husband bought himself *On Love*, which is not one of Stendhal's most famous books, and which he evidently didn't know. I only picked it up myself when I was writing the novel I read from tonight, but I couldn't get much out of it; I can't recall more than two or three passages that I found quite incisive. It's actually an amazingly rich selection of books that Jutta and her husband have standing against the long wall of their living room, almost a small library; next to consistently solid literature there's also cultural and political history, psychology, Marxism and a metre's worth of critical books on globalization; specialized medical literature seems to have a separate place in the study or the surgery.

When I discover *Minima Moralia*, I skip the section on furnishing with the line about wrong life and look for statements on modern marriage, which I recall appearing in a comparatively positive light; maybe I can find a quote of my own that will encourage Jutta. But on the very first pages, I encounter a passage that could hardly be more caustic: 'Marriage [ . . . ] usually serves today as a trick of self-preservation: the two conspirators deflect outward responsibility for their ill-doing to the other while in reality existing together in a murky swamp.'

Adorno's remarks on divorce in the following chapter, however, are even more withering:

> Divorce, even between good-natured, amiable, educated people, is apt to stir up a dust-cloud that covers and discolours all it touches. It is as if the sphere of intimacy, the unwatchful trust of shared life, is transformed into a malignant poison as soon as the relationship in which it flourished is broken off. Intimacy between people is forbearance, tolerance, refuge for idiosyncrasies. If dragged into the open, it reveals the element of weakness in it, and in a divorce such outward exposure is inevitable. It seizes the inventory of trust. Things which were once signs of loving care, images of reconciliation, breaking loose as independent values, show their evil, cold, pernicious side.

And Adorno doesn't even go into the aggressions that can arise when partners compete with each other for their children, to say nothing of the consequences for the children themselves, the scars of uncertainty and imagined guilt that are almost always imprinted on their souls by the separation of their parents. Here he only mentions the professors who, after separating, break into their wives' homes to steal objects from the desk, and also the well-financed ladies who denounce their husbands for tax evasion; but those are rather extreme examples, while I observe seemingly well-oiled separations among my friends and acquaintances whose amicable nature proves a farce for the children, and consequently the parents too.

But at least, in this section on divorce, I find the conciliatory remark on marriage that I still vaguely remembered, namely that it offers one of the last possibilities of forming human cells within universal inhumanity; but the universal takes revenge all the more inexorably when marriage breaks down, by subjugating love, which had seemingly been exempt from ownership-based thinking, all the more severely to the alienated orders of law and property:

> Just what was protected is cruelly requisitioned and exposed. The more 'generous' the couple had originally been, the less they thought of possessions and obligations, the more abominable becomes their humiliation. For it is precisely in the realm of the legally undefined that strife, defamation and endless conflicts of interest flourish.

I lower the book as tears fill my eyes. As if time had been turned back, I see myself with my former wife again, haggling with previously unimaginable resentment over how to divide up our shared account, discussing and even arguing over whatever pieces of furniture, which books belong to whom (as if one couldn't just buy them again), I can still hear myself screaming at her—I, who never raised my voice for my entire married life, which was probably part of the problem, this evasion of any conflict—cursing her in my outrage because I feel cheated over the days I am allowed to spend with my son, I hear both of us appearing before strangers, to a judge whom we only met that one time in our lives, making the most devious arguments, uttering genuine insults and revealing erotic intimacies. No, I'd better not read Jutta anything from *Minima Moralia*, and so I put the little white book that was once a bible for me back on the shelf.

There are two volumes of my own there, one of them a book about Neil Young, whom I couldn't get Jutta to like 30 years ago, and the novel I read from tonight. I quickly check if she marked any passages—sadly not, and the cover doesn't look particularly used either. Stendhal's treatise *On Love* is between *The Charterhouse of Parma* and *The Red and the Black*, which, unlike my novel, are visibly read; going by the stains, they were taken to the beach. Jutta brings the tea as I'm leafing through the treatise she earlier called 'obvious', or 'thin', or something like that. 'A woman of generous character will sacrifice her life a thousand times for her love, but will break with him forever over a question of pride—for the opening or shutting of a door.'

'Well, you could find something similar in any women's magazine,' says Jutta.

The editor will object that the book Jutta got me to sign couldn't already be on the shelf.

'Maybe she swiftly put it there when she got home,' I will say in my attempt to explain it.

The editor will be unconvinced that someone would enter their living room with a guest late in the evening and first of all sort their books, alphabetically too, and unnoticed, even though the visitor is sitting right in front of the shelf.

'Maybe I went for a quick pee,' I suggest, trying a different solution.

Now, no longer hiding his sarcasm, the editor will ask if he's really supposed to believe that Jutta dashed over to the shelf while I was doing my business. And he'll answer the question himself by saying that the toilet is not a site of literature.

'How should I know how the book ended up on the shelf!' I will exclaim, trying to shake off my editor, who, like a hunting dog, bites and doesn't let go whenever he catches me out for being careless. 'Maybe she has two copies.'

The editor will find the notion of someone buying my book twice too outlandish to consider. Instead, he will lecture me that anything can happen in a novel as long as it is made plausible to the reader. Then he'll take a deep breath before continuing with the ABC of writing: I should at least mention the fact that Jutta had put the book on the shelf so quickly, otherwise it would just look like a mistake.

'Yes, my God, yes!' I'll call out, drawing out the second 'yes' in annoyance. 'It doesn't always have to add up perfectly.'

As if I had attacked him personally, the editor will sink back into his movable backrest and mumble that in that case, his profession is superfluous. And, with an uncharacteristically drastic choice of words, he'll tell me that I can bloody well do it myself if it doesn't have to add up.

'It doesn't always add up in Proust either,' I will say, attempting to calm the editor and avoid saying what I've always thought of him: that he's an insufferable pedant.

The editor will ask what exactly I think doesn't add up in Proust, with such menace in his voice that I instantly regret invoking his idol.

'The information about times and places often don't add up,' I continue nonetheless, talking myself into a corner, and because the editor is smirking mockingly, adduce the example of a military greeting by Saint-Loup that, based on everything that happens in that time, would have to take at least two minutes. 'And that's impossible.'

With apparent interest, the editor will ask what scene I am referring to, and whether I am quite sure I read it properly.

'Yes, I'm absolutely sure!' I will insist and, because the editor considers all novelists incapable of close reading, refer to an essay that lists the inconsistencies in *Lost Time*; for example, the novelist observes a Lesbian orgy at the Vinteuils' from a hill and makes out not only the material of the blouses, but also the spit on the little photograph of the man of the house—from the hill! And then Proust makes the excuse that he was only a few centimetres away from the window and thus saw everything clearly. 'How can he be sitting on the hill and the window ledge at the same time?'

The editor will say nothing for two seconds in which nothing whatsoever happens around us, before swinging back towards me, very close to my face now, and whispering in the most spiteful way possible that I cannot seriously use Proust to excuse my sloppiness, that's really the limit.

'Okay, okay, okay,' I will say, ending the discussion at this point, because the novel I am writing offers entirely different ways to get back at him: I will, for example, be able to mention the smell that reaches me from the editor's mouth as he tears strips off me, yes, I'll just drag him out brutally into the public eye, given that editors like to operate in the shadows and parade their modesty like a trophy. Devoid of vanity to the point of self-denial, they don't even want to be named on the copyright page, so that the reader can imagine them as faithful servants, walking libraries and lean ascetics who live only for literature—but my editor is not like that, he's not like that at all, no; with his 150 kilogrammes he can hardly even walk. No wonder he spends his days grumbling over books; what else can a lard arse like that do except sit at his desk, and how else can a bookkeeper like that have fun than by spluttering triumphantly into his long, scruffy beard: 'Mistake! Nonsense! Unacceptable' as soon as he catches another lop-sided metaphor—which will prevent me from using any metaphors at all in the novel I am writing, because I just can't bear his spluttering any more: so no more apricots. He marks every grammatical error with a gusto that would befit a capital offence while munching away all day long, our modest servant of literature: he always has a sausage or a piece of cheese on his desk, as if I didn't notice the grease spots on my correction-covered manuscripts, just revolting, as I say, and eaten up by envy, like the sausage that—I kid you not—will be lying on the novel the next time I visit the publisher. Because, like all editors, he would have liked to be a novelist himself. But secondary virtues alone—punctuality, discipline and tidiness—are not enough to create literature.

'I'm very curious to know what you'll say,' I'll write in the novel before sending it to the editor. 'I think you're not a vain man.'

'98 kilogrammes', the editor will note in red in the margin, and cross out '150' with a thick line.

To find the more profound passages in *On Love*—I don't know if it's some kind of occupational solidarity that makes me want to defend a novelist even 200 years after his death—I've taken it to the couch with me, but Jutta doesn't seem interested in any further quotes and asks about my love life instead. She can't have noticed my sudden moment of intense emotion in front of the bookshelf—it passed too quickly, and I'd long regained my composure by the time she returned from the kitchen—or was there still a shadow of grief and melancholy on my face after all?

At any rate, if there is one thing I am good at, it's researching: revealing just enough in a conversation to make the other person lose their reservations about opening up to me. It's simply part of my occupation—especially on travels, but also in private situations, which I intuitively consider potential sources of material—that I switch to recording mode, as it were, I become purely an ear, an eye, to capture with or without a notepad what people do and say around me, just as a police officer sounds out a witness. Because yes, even though Jutta has only just brought the tea, it's already clear to me that our encounter will at least result in a novel, after my sugary fantasies about the night at her flat or my hotel room proved as laughable as the reader will have found them from the start: waking up in her arms, strolling through the town after breakfast and so forth. My God, to think that was genuinely going through my mind barely two hours ago: I was already wording the phone calls and letters with which we'd stay in touch, our reunion and the love that no longer arises in a second, but lasts forever. So I should hurry up and get back to the topic of her marriage, otherwise she'll be asking me about Islam next.

The immediate reason for getting married was that she wouldn't have been able to spend the night in his room at the Catholic community centre otherwise. He had presented her as a mere colleague, which was true enough for the first three days, and if anyone had found out that she started slipping into his bed on the fourth night, the priest would have put them both on a flight to the capital. Those were the circumstances in the Latin American provinces in the early nineties, and probably still are; the liberation preached by the priest certainly didn't relate to the body. Perhaps the young German could have rented a room somewhere else, but he would still have lost his job; the medical centre where he worked was run by the church, and its missionary purpose was not limited to the name, even though the doctors restricted themselves to healing the body. It suited her husband to treat the wedding as a mere formality, carried out more or less during their breakfast break at the registry office with the head doctor and ward nurse as witnesses, who had only been informed the day before; he didn't want any of the bourgeois nonsense and was glad to avoid a celebration with his German relatives. She told herself that she felt the same.

'And your parents?'

She called her parents after the ceremony, by which time he was already taking advantage of being in the capital and running errands, and was more or less able to calm them with the lie that they had married in church. And at least now she was no longer alone in the wilderness that they imagined Latin America to be, their son-in-law was a German and a doctor to boot, and, most importantly in the pious village near my birthplace in the early nineties, and probably still today: a Protestant.

'And his?'

His parents only learnt of the marriage when, as he happened to be in Germany, he brought the new daughter-in-law home with him. Even today, she's still ashamed of leaving out her parents, of forcing them to deal alone with the worries, the questions and the uncertainty about who their daughter's husband was, not to mention the village gossip they faced. Jutta says that I simply can't imagine how devout they all were back then, somehow suffocating, antiphysical in fact, possessed by fear and obedient to authority; but they were still such kind-hearted and caring people, especially her parents, whom, with that phone call, she had deprived of the most important celebration they could ever have in life. She has a completely different approach to religion, of course, Christian but not so fundamentalist, yet she can still hardly imagine one of her own children telling her on the phone, 'By the way, Mum, I got married.'

'But the worst thing was that I already knew very well back then, not just today, how awful that was for me parents.'

'But it was your wedding, not theirs,' I say to justify her. 'Your life, not theirs.'

'That's exactly what I thought at the time. Exactly the same, with those words: "my life, not theirs".'

'Right, so?'

'What a load of crap.'

What hurt her even more, though, was that her husband never mentioned the wedding when he called home, and only brought her along as a surprise guest when he visited; years later, he still introduced her to acquaintances only in passing, as if he was embarrassed of being married. And he probably was: it was embarrassing because his own life model was diametrically opposed to the petit bourgeois family.

'Didn't he want you?'

'I think neither of us really knew exactly what we wanted. He always says that was a sign of his love.'

'What do you mean?'

'The fact that he didn't hesitate to marry me, even though marriage wasn't on his list at all. He always says he felt from the start that I was the right woman for him. His brain just took a while to get it.'

'And, did you believe him?'

'I probably should've believed him.'

Jutta has gone back to wine by the time she asks the long-awaited question of whether I wouldn't rather go to bed instead of listening to her stories of marital frustration, which must seem trivial to someone like me. Holding my third cup of lemongrass tea, I claim that since the publication of—no, since writing the novel I read from tonight, I've been imagining I might see her again, so if she wants to go to bed she'll have to throw me out. I'm probably laying it on so thickly in the hope of making her a little more enthusiastic about our reunion, but Jutta simply enjoys talking to 'someone like me' for a change. She may only be the mayor of a small town, she says, but she still has to deal with the really big questions.

'Such as?' I ask, assuming that by 'someone like me' she means the novelist, reflecting daily on life, death and so forth with an archive of 5,000 years.

'Well, whether we're getting it right in Germany with integration,' Jutta says, making it clear that she considers my background more relevant than my literature.

That sort of thing really gets on my nerves, if I can at least be so frank in the novel I will be writing: this reduction of the stranger to his strangeness, whether it results in exclusion or, as so often in Jutta's and my generation, in paternalism. No denial of differences helps against such an idolatry of origin, no amount of effort to negate that otherness through zealous assimilation, for this only validates the assumptions that culture has always attempted to disprove—Culture with a capital C, I mean, literature, music, painting and most explicitly the writing of novels: it doesn't force humans into a template, but captures the inexhaustible and also contradictory, disconnected and thus unique quality of each personality. But fine, I suppose no woman in the world has to be confronted with a critique of identitarian thinking at one in the morning.

'Don't you have to get up very early tomorrow?' I ask, preferring to end the evening before she starts asking for my opinions.

'I can't sleep now anyway,' says Jutta, turning down my offer to leave.

'Because of the argument with your husband?'

'No, because of the joint. I never really smoke this late.'

'Oh, right.'

'I mean, we just had really good sex too,' she adds for no apparent reason.

'What?'

'Back then, I mean, when we got married, and I suppose after that too. That was always a factor with us, maybe more than with some other couples: sexually speaking, we were more or less stable.'

She can remember each of the three nights in which she crept through the dark hall of the Catholic community centre. The first night, they didn't sleep together yet, just lay stretched out on the bed, whispering like schoolchildren . . .

'About what?'

'It sounds a bit ridiculous now, but it's actually true: usually about the revolution.'

. . . and when she suddenly felt his hand on her hand in the middle of the conversation, it seemed so natural that she continued her sentence after an exchange of glances. Only a little later she stood up because she wanted to let him sleep, thought his days were exhausting enough, even though he insisted he wasn't tired; they shared a farewell kiss, and that was it. But that touching of hands and the brief, fleeting kiss already held the promise of all the love she would feel.

'And the second night?'

'Things went really fast then: I'd hardly arrived before we were already undressed. It went a bit too fast.'

And yet the failure that he couldn't help feeling as a man, as well as a degree of disappointment and the initial speechlessness after what they had deliberately delayed yesterday had now ended grotesquely—this undeniable, self-evident letdown only bound them closer together. The fact that she found the only right words for the situation—humorous words—added gratitude to his admiration. And she found it sweet how he exaggerated his contrition.

'And the third?'

'From the third night, we made love.'

She sees now that she was the one who was quick, too quick in fitting her love into a mould, wanting to seal it with a visible bond. Twenty years ago . . .

'You've been together that long!'

'Twenty-three, to be precise.'

. . . everything seemed to happen by itself, and the worry that the priest might hear her at night in the hallway of the Catholic community centre, or even in her lover's bed, wasn't just a pretext—at first it was just so she could sleep in his room, honestly!—Jutta assures me in her self-deception, even twenty-three years later. How many nights did this even affect, how often did she actually fly to the jungle, such that sharing a room would be a reason to get married? He usually visited her in the capital, where no one cared about a marriage certificate.

'But didn't you work together in the jungle?' I ask.

'No, what gave you that idea?'

I don't know either what gave me that idea, I suppose I had an image of the two lovers in the Amazon . . .

'Ecuador is 5,000 kilometres away from the Amazon.'

'Well, then some other place in the jungle.'

. . . flying from one settlement to the next. Her husband did actually find a position at her hospital, and the purpose of the marriage certificate was served during another two visits, eight nights in all, when they could just as easily have crept secretly into his room. They didn't make any noise during sex anyway.

There is a reflection by Proust that perhaps explains the asynchronicity lamented by Jutta with regard to her husband's love for her. While the youth dreams of winning the heart of the woman he is in love with, the man may be content with the feeling that he possesses a woman's heart in order to make her love him.

At this time of life one has already been wounded many times by love; it no longer evolves solely in accordance with its own unknown and inevitable laws, before our astonished and passive heart. We come to its aid, we distort it with memory, with suggestion. Recognising one of its symptoms, we recall and revive the others. Since we know its song, engraved in us in its entirety, we do not need a woman to repeat the beginning of it—filled with the admiration that beauty inspires—in order to find out what comes after. And if she begins in the middle—where the two hearts come together, where it sings of living only for each other—we are accustomed enough to this music to join our partner right away in the passage where she is waiting for us.

Fortunately I will only recall this passage while writing the novel the reader is holding, otherwise I would stand up now to get the first volume of *Lost Time*, which I have discovered complete on the shelf, and would once again read Jutta the insights of a wiser—no, of the most knowledgeable of all novelists.

Perhaps the reader will be bothered by the quotations that intermittently appear throughout this story, will find them superfluous, too eager to appear educated, or narratively false, since I can indeed see the shelf from my seat on the couch, but clearly don't actually get up every few minutes to read to Jutta from a book. After justifying the previous book, it's embarrassing to do so now with the novel I'm about to write, especially after announcing that the references to French literature would be self-explanatory. But aren't novelists all somehow lovers, pining away—if only posthumously—for you, the reader, and isn't folly a part of love? Yes, if I can talk to you like a friend, with an intimacy that I often find unpleasant in daily life, quite unbearable in adverts: you, dear reader, because I cannot help wishing that you could be a friend, a close and forgiving person, so that I can write, in however literary a form, about what's important to me now.

Like someone in love who risks everything by revealing his intentions, I will explain that the digressions on literary history are supposed to break up the coherence of my story, which only comes about after the event. After all, it is not as if only Jutta and I exist, maybe her husband too, upstairs in the study, and the children in their beds—all three, or has the eldest already left home? I still haven't asked her—as if I were only paying attention to her, listening only to her words, gestures, glances, her person, as if I were one with the present that I share with her. It's impossible to be one, except perhaps in ecstasies such as lovemaking, as Jutta would put it, listening to music or prayer; or in ecstasies of overwhelming distress, when we have just learnt of the death of someone beloved or have been left by our lover, and even in our need, we still wonder where the wax spot on the table came from that we happen to be staring at, or who that might be calling us on the phone. We are not even one in distress; if anything, only in a state of utmost rapture, and then only for a few seconds that we precisely cannot measure, whereas we are simultaneously in countless different states at all other times.

To name only the most obvious examples, my thoughts often drift (even though I claim to be in receptive mode) to my own son, to my former wife—sure, that may still relate to Jutta, who is sitting facing me—but also tonight's reading, for example, the plans for the next summer holidays, the daily news, the book I'm currently working on—not the novel the reader is holding, I should point out, but one that will long have been published by then—I see the DVDs on the floor and the face of an actor reminds me of the film with him that I watched, and of the world-weary friend who accompanied me; of particular statements made at the pub afterwards, the unknown woman standing next to me at the pub while I appeared to be concentrating on the conversation, how that friend is doing now and the text message I plan to send him first thing tomorrow morning. And so on, on and on. Or the banal yet justified question of every child since the invention of cinema: doesn't the hero ever need the toilet? While Jutta tells me of her rapture and her distress, I wait for the sentence to end so that I can disappear briefly without seeming impolite or disinterested, and once I start thinking about bladders, I automatically think of . . . and so on, on and on, if I wanted to follow all the associations, feelings, sounds, observations, thoughts, impressions, ideas, daydreams and so forth—a never-ending experience just in this one situation, where Jutta takes me for an especially empathetic listener.

And it's no different for her: she's also somewhere else at the same time, even someone else, she's not just the former school-yard sweetheart and conflicted wife I see sitting opposite me, but simultaneously has all sorts of things going through her mind and her body—I can tell just from her glances at the display of the smartphone on the coffee table, even when she doesn't check what's in the messages that occasionally flash up, and all the more when she does read them in parallel. I'll block all of that out of my mind, because the bookshelf is a more interesting digression and literary history is relatively coherent. After all, a reader's attention always drifts too, or they might even reach for a different novel in the middle. In any case, it doesn't tell us very much when a novelist tells us their intentions; you wouldn't trust a lover announcing their plans either.

Jutta can't decide if she's romanticizing the start of her marriage up to the birth of their first son . . .

'30 minus 23 minus 2 or 3', I miscalculate mentally, making less than two years after our schoolyard romance: how young she was.

. . . if her husband was really so attentive, if they always made love so passionately, if there were never arguments, not even differences of opinion. Their relationship can't possibly have been so consistently happy and harmonious, she knows that, but she can only remember the doubts, conflicts and annoyances vaguely at best; it's all in a kind of haze, those early days, which her memory seems to have cleansed of all unwanted feelings and disturbing situations in order to find the present more disappointing.

'Anyway, I was totally infatuated: I must've just thought he was great, everything about him.'

Of course, in retrospect there are aspects of his manner, his opinions, his behaviour that she doesn't just find silly now, but even disapproves of or firmly rejects, things that were there from the start, and when she picks up old photos, she doesn't even think he looked like such a dream.

'Robert Redford, you said.'

But back then, if she's honest, she liked everything about him, especially his quirks. As devoted as she was to him, she would probably—at least, she can't dismiss it as pathological when she reads about such fatal emotions—she would probably still have taken his side if he had been a fraud, or even beaten her.

'But he wasn't a fraud and he didn't beat you, I assume: he was evidently a really good guy, someone who wanted to help, who dedicated himself to an important cause.'

'Well sure, that's why our marriage has lasted: there was never much to hold against him, objectively speaking. Sometimes I almost wished I would wake up and find a monster next to me; then I could just have left. But there wasn't a monster, there was exactly that good guy. But I still woke up next to him.

Love in its pure form can only exist as longing. If there's one basic motif in literary tradition that runs through Jutta's bookshelf, it's the disillusionment that inevitably results from fulfilment. Already in *Camille*, the central book on a romantic love that defies all conventions, the aim of the young, wealthy Armand is not to sleep with the beautiful courtesan Marguerite; that would be too easy. No, his goal is to win her heart after she has laughed at him. That is, love sets in at the moment she torments him with her disdain, and thus becomes unattainable. And Alexandre Dumas, who wrote this successful novel, himself refers to earlier authors who already knew the motif. A certain Alphonse Karr, for example, who is completely unknown to me, tells of a man who stalks an elegant lady with whom he believes he has fallen in love.

> As he is dreaming of the things he would do to possess her, she stops him at a street corner and asks if he would like to come upstairs with her.
> He turns his head away, crosses the street and returns home sadly.

Essentially, all premodern love stories describe desire, not the actual union, much less the cohabitation of two lovers, their marriage and how they grow old side by side. In dramas, the lovers die before they find each other, and the fairy tale stops as soon as they have—and they only live happily ever after because they don't die. Only with bourgeois marriage does literature begin to describe love as a long-term relationship. At the very moment it fulfils itself it already becomes diluted, however unconsciously and temporarily—no, it doesn't necessarily fade away; on the contrary, in the best, unfortunately rare case, it can become firmer and more enduring after cooling off—because it loses that aspect of the unimaginable, the ungraspable and, in a sense, its transcendence. Proust writes,

> And the mind is not even at liberty to remake its own earlier state, so as to compare it with the present one: the new acquaintance we have just made, the memory of those first unexpected moments, the words we have heard spoken, blocking the entrance to our conscious-ness, and commanding the exits from memory much more than those from imagination, act backwards against our past, which we can no longer see without their presence in it, rather than acting forwards on the still unoccupied shape of our future.

At the church congress before last—no idea what makes Jutta think of that now, and tell me of all people—she met a former schoolmate who confessed to having been desperately in love with her. Now, like her, he has a family, has children who still live at home, and, as a bishop, holds public office.

'A bishop?' I ask incredulously.

'Yes,' Jutta says with a mischievous laugh, 'and if you Google where he was born, you'll know who it is straight away.'

He could hardly believe that she hadn't noticed his affection. Despite not having any hope, because she was 'going with' an older boy, as we said innocently 30 years ago, he had confessed his love, or at least shown it openly, and all their closer friends knew about his misfortune; even her best friend, whom he often turned to, only for her to tear the renewed hope from his heart again. Jutta suspects that she blocked out any awareness of his feelings, or didn't want to believe them, so that they could remain friends. This schoolmate was different from her other friends; he not only came from one of the strictly religious villages in the area, like her, but also went to church on Sundays, whereas she was already a regular visitor at the squat behind the train station. He was intelligent and caring, he'd always been top of the class, and he actually wasn't bad-looking if she imagined him without the ironed shirt and parted hair. And whenever they got into conversation, either at one of their homes or, more often, on their walks, almost hikes through the woods, where they almost got lost deliberately, she was sometimes struck by how previous their intimacy was. They probably didn't meet up as often as she remembered, and those walks in particular imprinted themselves on her memory more deeply than some romantic relationships. She can hardly explain to herself why she never thought of touching the boy in anything more than a friendly way; probably he just didn't fit the idea she had of how a lover should be.

'What age was that?'

'We must have been 17 or 18.'

'So it was before our time?'

As absurd as it is, I feel relieved 30 years later to know that she wasn't unfaithful with a friend or admirer during the week that I was her lover.

'And do you know what happened?'

'When?'

'Well, at the church congress.'

'No,' I reply unsuspectingly.

'I totally fell in love.'

Jutta dreamt of him in her hotel bed—and they weren't exactly pious dreams, she says, but wild sexual fantasies. When she woke up she was too aroused to go back to sleep, and then she was kept awake by bafflement at these unmistakable symptoms of infatuation, which she didn't think she could still experience at her age. In the next days and weeks she constantly thought about her old schoolmate who was now a bishop, imagining both an affair and, allowing for all possibilities, even a new marriage.

'And then?' I ask.

'Nothing,' Jutta replies.

'What do you mean, nothing?'

'I didn't tell him.'

While I'm still thinking about why she didn't respond to the bishop's confession—it needn't have led to an affair, I would have told Jutta, let alone a marriage, but just voicing one's desire makes a relationship richer—she changes the subject again and asks what I think of the new Houellebecq, which all of Europe has been talking about since the Paris terror attacks.

'I haven't read it,' I reply, hoping she won't draw me into a conversation about the Islamization of the West.

'But why not?' Jutta continues, unfortunately.

I feel my anger rising, and it grows even stronger for being noticed.

'You've got Stendhal, Proust, Balzac, Zola and Flaubert on your shelf, Baudelaire and Céline too, and you ask me about Houellebecq?'

'One doesn't have to like him, but one should at least know him, don't you think?'

'But why?'

'Because it's extremely relevant.'

'For whom?'

'Well, for you, I thought.'

'Why?'

'Because it's precisely about . . . ' she begins, then suddenly gets up and goes to the shelf, presumably to get the book.

'You don't have to read it to me,' I try to stop her, 'I know what's in there.'

'I thought you hadn't read it,' Jutta teases while looking on the shelf for authors beginning with H.

'Well, no . . . '

I avert my gaze and console myself with the fact that it's time to return to the hotel anyway, and then Jutta puts me out of my misery with the news that she can't find the new Houellebecq; probably her husband's reading it at the moment. Instead, she's holding a book that usually stands directly next to H:

'Do you know Julien Green?'

I will think about whether to put her love in a chronology, or at least a reasonably visible order, but ultimately decide to write the novel with the same kinds of omissions, anticipations and later additions that appear whenever people tell stories. Having stumbled on Julien Green by chance while searching for Houellebecq, Jutta returns to describing how devotedly she initially followed her husband. To be honest, I find it hard to see any connection between her and the 16-year-old Adrienne Mesurat, who, for no apparent reason, falls for a doctor 30 years her senior who has moved into the neighbourhood when she briefly catches sight of him in the street as he goes past in his carriage.

Adrienne drives her older, sick sister out of the house just so that she can move into her room, which overlooks the doctor's house; she even kills her father, half accidentally and half intentionally, when he tries to put an end to her passion; she writes anonymous love letters to the doctor and finally faints in order to be treated by him. It's the most reckless, unrealistic, hopeless, one-sided and—because the doctor, whom Adrienne has only seen in passing, turns out to be a sickly, emaciated, bookish oddball—un-erotic love ever described in modern literature. There's nothing that the two have in common, nothing that explains Adrienne's feelings, nor anything that could attract the doctor to her. It's really something like a love for a very distant, forbidding, perhaps not even existent God, certainly a religious fervour, albeit of the darkest kind. 'You don't love me,' the doctor says, 'That's impossible.' Jutta, on the other hand, encountered a man who . . .

'What's he doing at the moment?'

'Still busy with the accounts, knowing him.'

. . . whose age, profession, life situation, interests, goals, opinions, looks and so forth aligned with her in an almost uncanny way, a man with whom she shared not only her background and her academic qualification, but also her confession, which was taken particularly seriously in her parents' house. However unaware she may have been of the socially appropriate nature of this love, however firmly she believed she was ignoring familial dictates—feelings are always unconsciously influenced by reasons that are shockingly pragmatic when viewed in the cold light of day, especially when the goal is to start a family sooner or later. Jutta's love wasn't just possible; after completing her studies, alone in a foreign land and starting a new phase of her life, it was consistent, almost logical. She would have fallen in love with any other man with roughly the same attributes who had appeared in the same place, at the same time. 'You set your mind on this one day when you were lonely,' the doctor says to Adrienne in an attempt to dissuade her from her love, 'when you were tormented by boredom.'

> 'You could just as easily have loved someone else. Assume someone other than myself had gone past you in his carriage on the day you told me about earlier, a young man perhaps . . . '
> 'Why should I assume all that?' Adrienne replies. 'Even if what you say is true, it changes nothing.'

For Jutta, who goes to church on Sundays whenever she can, it's almost a religious matter whether there could have been a different man standing at the exit of that provincial Latin American airport—not someone completely different, she's realistic enough to see that, not the attendant scrubbing the terminal, not an older or totally ugly man, probably not a local, as interested as she was in the country; but any other reasonably good-looking young aid worker with a German or at least Western-style background. She refuses to believe it: would that other man have searched for her with the same shy gaze and identified himself from behind the barrier with the same smile? Would he have exhibited his monosyllabic manner just as obviously yet paid her a compliment in the third sentence, one that she would still remember in its tonal nuances a quarter-century later? She had already fallen in love by then, she claims, during that space of roughly 60 seconds after their eyes met and he took her rucksack—and she knew almost nothing about him at that point, barely more than the fact that he wasn't an attendant, old or ugly, and not a local either.

'But that's total nonsense,' I interject. 'You already knew all sorts of things about him when you met.'

'Like what?'

'That he was a doctor, that he was young, that he was taking care of Indigenous people, that he was leading a life you thought was great.'

'Yes, but that alone doesn't explain anything. It was that gaze too.'

'Right, the gaze.'

Sure, the children were the most important reason to be reconciled with each other time and again, more exhausted and disillusioned after every fight, until reconciliation amounted to accepting once again what couldn't be changed. Nonetheless, there was another factor, the aforementioned religious motive. No, Jutta doesn't mean the biblical condemnation of divorce; her parents' view that one shouldn't separate was at most an unconscious influence. It was more about a principle that was fundamental to Jutta's whole idea of religion: trust in God.

'Trust in God?' I ask, just to be sure.

' "Not a single sparrow will fall to the ground apart from the will of your Father"—that's how I was brought up, it was kind of an extreme environment.'

She believed that her life, her husband's life, her children's life and human life in general, just like every other form of life, is governed by a destiny that isn't necessarily known to the individual. Yes, it's precisely when it's unknown that we have to accept life, because it's guided by a higher hand: 'your will be done', that's really the essence of all religiosity.

'Now you're attributing your own thoughts to me,' Jutta will say when she reads the novel.

'That's not true,' I will insist. 'You really did say that about the sparrow.'

However often she cried into her pillow, however many days, sometimes weeks she spoke to her husband only to make the most necessary arrangements, always hoping that the right course of action would become apparent by itself, whether it was a continuation of this life or the beginning of an entirely new life—she would have accepted it either way. Unlike for her parents, divorce was very much an option for her. But once they're speaking again, touches soon follow and their bodies join with new passion after almost every argument, she's relieved that the family—and that's what all this is about, when there are children it's never just about the husband or the wife—is still intact.

'I thought you didn't argue any more?' I comment with a hint of scepticism.

'I mean, he does love me,' Jutta replies, as if I'd asked a different question. 'And I do know that.'

But each reconciliation raises the cost that a separation would have after the next quarrel, because then everything—even longer perseverance, even greater pain, even more frequent compromise—would have been in vain. Breaking up after a few years, even with children, as serious as that always is—it happens. But if half of one's life turned out to have been a mistake, Jutta would have just as little faith in the other half.

She's not actually speaking to me. At least slightly intoxicated by wine, marijuana and a fatigue that has given way to an easy, relaxed mood, she's talking to herself, questioning herself, exposing herself to herself, provoking herself, saying a mixture of disjointed and sentimental things, coming up with explanations like her faith in God that she probably wouldn't believe herself in the cold light of day, while saying nothing about the pragmatic considerations that undoubtedly also played a part, all the circumstances that would result from a divorce, such as the flat she'd have to look for and furnish from scratch—but when? And she's still so attached to the old villa; and the double costs, or the lonely weekends when the children are with her husband, or even out of the house, and where would she go on holiday? Out here in the country, who know when she'd find someone to go with her, let alone a new love? But each time she probably says to herself that she shouldn't be in a marriage for such shallow reasons, and keeps waiting for a feeling that would finally be unequivocal, not only in that moment, but also the following day and the following week.

Our feelings are in conflict, I know it so well from my own experience—a constant, increasingly agonizing and seemingly intractable conflict—when two people are shackled to each other by children, through a shared everyday life and in their shared bed; however many wounds they inevitably inflict on each other when their love turns into coexistence, however many misunderstandings arise when one is in constant dialogue, time—the very fact of long and ever longer time—at once lends constancy to love, steels it against the moods that always come and go. With each crisis they overcome, each experience of happiness, each stroke of fate and, above all, with increasing habituation, time creates the seemingly unbreakable bond and supplies the reasons that were initially more imagined than real. What began as a chance meeting, and Jutta's marriage was ultimately just as coincidental as Adrienne's encounter with the doctor, only reveals over time whether it was a necessity or a mistake—but which of the two was it? There are so many arguments against that person, but no proof that another would be any better.

I wouldn't notice the way she occasionally says the opposite of what she said a moment earlier if I weren't in the aforementioned receptive mode. Now it's the quarrelling in her marriage that continues to happen or doesn't even happen any more; before that it was the moment when she felt more than just falling in love, namely the certainty that the stranger was her future husband: she already experienced it when she arrived in the provincial town, or maybe it was only in the jungle, when he laughed off the tribulations like the sweat he wiped from his brow. Or was it at night at the community centre, and if so, was it during the first kiss, their failed union or their ecstatic one? Or was it only when she looked back on the week on the flight back to the capital? Those are more than just inconsistencies; every one of those images of early love that she remembers shines as bright for a lifetime as if it were the source of the remaining light. Maybe they all have a nimbus of uniqueness because remarkably few images have stayed in her memory—if she adds up how many hours and days they spent together in the jungle.

Immediately another memory returns, contradicting a different one without that really mattering: before he took her hand on the bed in the middle of their conversation, and it seemed so natural that she only interrupted her sentence for a brief exchange of glances, they had already touched. It was a few hours earlier on the veranda, with the priest next to them in conversation with the local doctor, the nurses and a few churchgoers. In the dark, no one could see him place his hand on hers; no one even paid attention to the two young Germans. And yet she hastily pulled her hand away, before being shocked that she had rejected him. She claims—knowing that it's an exaggeration, but what memory of love isn't?—that she heard her heart beating as she waited to see if the hand would return to hers.

Novelist that I am, I can't help thinking of the famous scene from Stendhal's *The Red and the Black*, one I am sure Jutta also knows; her copy shows unmistakable traces of holiday reading, at least: when the young Latin teacher Julien—on the veranda at night, while the others are speaking!—touches the hand of Madame de Rênal, his student's mother. The beloved, despite returning Julien's feelings, immediately withdraws her hand. Henceforth it is no longer desire that drives Julien, but rather the ambition not to be rejected. When his hand comes to rest on hers, joy flows through his soul, for a terrible agony has ended; but that feeling has nothing to do with love, Stendhal claims, but is more of a sporting triumph.

'All that excitement just because you wanted to hold hands with him?' I ask, to avoid bringing up Stendhal. 'You can't have been that inexperienced.'

'But somehow every new love feels like a first time, doesn't it?'

'Well well,' I say, trying out a paternal tone. 'And despite being such an innocent, you crept into his room that same night?'

'Yes, because he hadn't put his hand back on mine on the veranda.'

So the fact that they made love, which is evidently Jutta's usual way of describing sex, was more of a sporting triumph for her too.

The plan was for her to go and live with him in the jungle, but first she had to do her elective at a hospital that would be recognized as adequate in Europe, and then there'd need to be a vacancy for a doctor at the medical centre. Living purely off his salary, which was just the usual amount in the area, was out of the question given their extra expenses—even just the flights to the capital for essential supplies, and to Germany at Christmas. Even two incomes wouldn't have been enough, at least, not with the children that she'd imagined from the start. But living in the jungle with children wasn't an option anyway. In other words, it had always been an illusion that they'd share their daily bread with the local helpers.

When it transpired that she couldn't move in with him, he was faced with the choice between continuing the life that satisfied him without her, or starting a life with her that he rejected. He never brought it up. But today she realizes . . .

'If only I'd seen it earlier!'

. . . how much he gave up for her.

She understands the sacrifice he made, though she's also right that he would have given up working in the jungle anyway, as the payment wasn't even enough for decent health insurance, let alone a pension. For him, it was a sacrifice that she didn't acknowledge.

I shouldn't think they hadn't tried. They tried it several times. No, not being together, they've been trying that half their lives. Tried to separate. Twice he'd spent weeks sleeping at the surgery, and one time she'd already signed the rental contract for a flat. They both hired lawyers, and together they informed both their children and their parents that they would begin the one-year separation that was required for divorce, and would take it very seriously; one doesn't just give up something as precious as three children who've turned out happy, self-confident and decent, Jutta keeps emphasizing, as if to justify herself, an everyday life that runs like clockwork despite two stressful professions, and agreement on the things that come up in marriage counselling multiple choice tests—what to do with the parents if they need help? Or the fact that their relatives get on and they're more than just five people: they're the centre of one big, harmonious unit. And to round it off: not one argument about money in all these years, and the sexual desire is still there. No, says Jutta, as if to convince herself, having so much in common isn't something to take for granted; and yet she constantly hears a voice (a diabolical voice, she fears) whispering in her ear that there's something missing from this web of professional life, children, neigh-bourhood, grandparents and successful daily routines, something that she in particular misses: the little moments of affection, the conversations—he's just not interested!—him spending time with her without chasing her through the Alps, nothing special, like—she can't think of a better example—accompanying her just once to the parish fair, which admittedly isn't as exciting as holidaying in Brokdorf, simply to make her happy, and the parishioners aren't as stuffy as all that. But as soon as he hears the word 'church' he puts on his running shoes as a matter of principle, and if he's not training for a marathon then he goes mountain biking, excusing himself in a reproachful tone that religion just isn't his thing. Or falling asleep together, falling asleep arm in arm, which happens so rarely because he gets by with far less sleep than she does, then reads a book, goes jogging at 10 p.m., or sits down at the computer to do the books, if he's not looking for quite different things on the internet, who knows what he gets up to. Nonetheless, both separation years ended before they'd started, though she can't really say why.

'She explained it herself,' the editor will say as we go through this novel in his office.

'What?' I'll ask.

'Why they stayed together.'

'She just explained what keeps them together, in spite of everything.'

'Yes, and that's exactly what love is.'

'The children, the house, the daily routine, their parents?'

'Yes, exactly that.'

'That's just the glue.'

'No, that's not just glue.'

'If it were love, they'd stay together without children, house and parents too.'

'But love isn't some entity that somehow exists independently of life.'

'What then?'

'It's the life one shares.'

'So, flat-sharing plus sex.'

'Plus children, family firm, holidays, emergency calls, nursing service, terminal care, going out for a pizza and so on.'

'Then one could just get oneself a contract partner.'

'You don't do all that without love.'

'People did it in the past too, without love.'

'According to you.'

'According to me.'

'But you don't even know what love is.'

'No.'

And then? Then he accepted her chief physician's offer to work at the clinic in the capital. Not for long, and he became so resentful about treating the propertied class that he started applying to aid agencies, despite his fierce criticism of the industry. Intentionally or not, she was soon pregnant. Just in time for the birth, he was accepted for an executive position in Bolivia that came with a company car, house and foreign allowance. At least the poor there were just as grateful for their treatment as the people in the Ecuadorian jungle, whatever their doctor was making. Not that Jutta's husband had imagined he could change the system from within—in his view, her view and mine too, imperialism itself created the hardship from whose alleviation it drew profit; but he certainly turned the office upside down, Jutta recounted proudly despite their marital crisis, eroding hierarchies, reallocating funds, limiting his privileges and those of his staff, setting up councils in the villages, as well as advancing education and women's rights. No, he didn't propagate revolution as the best medicine any more, but certainly a more just society. At home too, they shared their table with the servants.

'You had servants?'

'We couldn't really throw them out.'

Twenty years later, Jutta finds it hard to say if she was happy in Bolivia. Her memories are dominated by a feeling of being overwhelmed: overwhelmed by the baby, by the big house, by the servants, frustrated by the search for a job of her own and unstoppable in her eagerness to work as a doctor instead of just being the wife, without realizing that maybe it was precisely in her ambition that she was following him—that she wanted to emulate him, was competing with him. She finds it completely crazy: instead of devoting herself to the baby and enjoying the first one or two years as a hiatus, as well as enjoying the unaccustomed luxury . . .

'Chauffeur, maidservant, pool,' Jutta lists, and finds it perverse for aid workers to live in such luxury.

. . . and discovering the country at her leisure, she weaned her children much too early and organized the best possible childcare, extending to a detailed dietary plan that used only the healthiest and most toxin-free ingredients, preferably home grown, in order to travel to the villages with her husband, in constant worry—after all, there were no mobile phones back then that she could have used to call home. She told herself that his work was important, that he was doing good, and she could hardly blame him for his commitment. At the same time, it nagged at her that despite all her attempts, she remained the woman by his side—especially in the villages, because without a position, and thus insurance coverage, she could only treat the less severe cases and was practically responsible for the social work, the conversations among women, who often didn't understand Jutta's aims because they had more pressing concerns than equal rights. 'What rights?' the women often asked in response. But whom could she have spoken to about her dissatisfaction?

So new to the country, there was no one except her husband, and he would have replied . . .

'And he wouldn't have been wrong,' she now admits.

. . . that he was living a life with a secretary, meetings and Oktoberfest at the German embassy purely for her sake. At least, she thought that was what he would've said. The conflicts began, and they're still explained with the wrong reasons today—not just arbitrary reasons, not just trivial reasons, but the wrong reasons, so that even the reconciliation alternately initiated by him and by her is misleading. She sees it very coolly today: essentially it was about domination, about who decides and who follows. The pecking order of her parents' generation no longer applied, yet she found herself in the role of a mother and was supposed to accept him as the provider. The one thing she couldn't explain to herself, to anyone—maybe a therapist, but she'd rather not confide in a therapist out here in the country— was why she felt this anger towards him, why she fell in love with another man, why more and more things about her husband bothered her with each passing year, yet she nonetheless became jealous for the most trivial reasons. At first I don't believe her, and say that jealousy somehow doesn't chime with her character, with someone so independent, but Jutta replies that she finds it awful herself. Then she watches herself from the outside, watches as she turns into a pubescent, angry girl. Alright, I think to myself, then maybe there's a reason for it, and ask who the object of her jealousy is.

She's barely spoken a word before I want to cry out: please, no! It can't be that trivial, it's the soap opera classic: her husband has a new receptionist, not even 30 years old, a ray of sunshine who put everyone in a good mood from day one and, Jutta admits without prejudice, put the surgery in order. If it were that well ordered, her husband wouldn't have to do the accounts at night, I interject. In reality, I want to reassure her that she really doesn't need to worry about a receptionist, she receives so many compliments herself that it gets on her nerves, and she certainly doesn't lack self-confidence. She tells herself a thousand times that the new receptionist is no competition for her, and she can hardly imagine the logistics of an affair anyway—when and where would it happen? Surely not at work, and in the evenings he always does his training, assuming he's not in his study. She knows she's acting out *Desperate Housewives*, but she just can't shake off her role, and she can't accuse her husband or the receptionist of anything, so she doesn't bring it up; but she senses how the thought that there might be something after all is eating her up, because twice, a long time ago, something completely unexpected happened, and the women weren't even young, whereas the receptionist—alright, he's not likely to discuss the murderousness of capitalism with her, but she's blonde, blonde and thick as a brick. Now Jutta's starting to get mean, because if the receptionist were really thick as a brick, she'd hardly be able to organize things so well at the surgery, and on top of that—now we're getting to the heart of it—she does sports as well.

When her husband leaves the house in his tennis gear, Jutta does sometimes wonder whether he's really going to the tennis court, and last year she even went as far as dropping in at the tennis club just to find out if her husband was playing, and with whom. But of course it was a man on the court with him, with no trace of the receptionist in sight. But the tennis warden was happy about the rare visit and invited the mayor to participate in the indoor tournament. She knows very well that she's getting old, probably already finished her menopause, and those three excess pounds that have resisted every diet—while he keeps his body in shape so that young women will be impressed by more than just his social status.

'How arsey is that?' Jutta will say in disbelief when she sees what I conclude from her jealousy, which was not easy for her to admit.

'Well, if that's how it was,' the editor will say, agreeing with me for once. 'She could find something similar in her copy of *Woman's World*.'

'I don't read stuff like that,' Jutta will ask me to pass on to the editor.

'I just said it to make you aware of the level your novel is stooping to,' the editor will say, naturally taking the opportunity for a swipe at me.

Sure, obviously someone who only knows about love from books would never go below his level.

Stendhal describes Julien's second great love—Mathilde, who is his own age—as an even fiercer competition: she awakens his feelings by rejecting him, and he wins her over by withdrawing, in constant alternation. This culminates—and that is how he finally triumphs—in his following point by point, against his instincts and all his own feelings, a battle plan that an experienced friend has given him. Even the love letters he writes to another woman to arouse Mathilde's jealousy are copied word for word from his friend. Everything that follows from this start, especially the ultimate cooling of Julien's emotions and the return of Madame de Rênal in his death cell, points to the insight that love remains a secret in spite of everything. It's only the beginning of the love affair itself, however much space Stendhal devotes to it, that I always found silly—though not unrelated to the often-harmful dynamic of defensiveness and heightened desire that arises between two lovers, it seems too much like a caricature. Please, not quite so trivial! I kept thinking while reading it, the same way I wanted to call out to Jutta before.

Maybe I was wrong, and not only while reading. Maybe the secret of love lies, among other things, in the fact that it's far simpler than we ourselves believe, and simpler than writers would have us think, all of them except for Stendhal. Maybe we also copy letters that have been sent a thousand times. Maybe it's really only about—no, not only, but to a considerable extent, especially in the transition from infatuation to lasting love, when the terms are set for the next years and decades—maybe it's genuinely about top and bottom, ruling and following, refusal and desire, cruelty and pleasure; maybe that's true of every human relationship, though nowhere else is it wrapped in such delightful words and tender gestures as between two lovers. I don't know if it's because of Stendhal, or even Jutta, who's now telling me about the social upheavals in Bolivia, but I find myself wondering why modernity, which began to erode fixed gender roles, at once saw the emergence of sadomasochism as a form of eroticism—and why today in particular, when gender equality has established itself, at least in the public consciousness, sadomasochism has become a kind of national sport, especially among the affluent. Though strictly speaking, it's not sadism that became a mass phenomenon in prosperous Western societies so much as the desire to serve, to humiliate oneself, to expose oneself to pain and negate our overdeveloped ego; by now, men in particular probably spend more money for the privilege of being dominated by a woman than for ordinary prostitution, which preserves the old power relations, and women daydream unabashedly about *Fifty Shades of Grey* on the metro. And yet we in particular have paraded equality like an article of faith; Jutta's West German generation, which I also belong to, has preached it at conferences and demonstrations, in books, parties, election campaigns, committees, research reports, curricula, companies, in all the media, even in the churches. We've even eroded hierarchies in the national football team, just as Jutta's husband tried to do at his office. My thoughts wander as Jutta rails against imperialism once again.

To get her onto a different topic, I ask—after something of a lead up, clearing my throat a few times—how things are going for her sexually. After all, she mentioned that she and her husband are remarkably stable in this regard:

'That reflects positively on your marriage, doesn't it?'

'Yes, that's always been a factor,' she says, and repeats a phrase reminiscent of economics or even mathematics: 'But we're working on it too.'

'What do you mean, you're working on it?'

'Well, we approach it very openly,' says Jutta, with the familiar knowing smirk that treats me like the younger, inexperienced, naive one.

Evidently she's expecting me to react awkwardly, or more than that: she sees what I'm getting at and thinks, alright, if that's what he wants.

'You mean you have an open relationship?' I ask cautiously.

'No, we do pretty much do it together,' explains Jutta, 'but not just the usual things.'

Novelist that I am, I immediately imagine revels like those described by Arthur Schnitzler, which are all the more uninhibited in the provinces; or, to return to my earlier train of thought, parties like those in de Sade, Jutta playing the role of the leather-clad dominatrix in this other life, her husband a whimpering puppy, presumably with racks and instruments of torture in the basement. But Jutta is the mayor of this little town, and her husband runs a thriving surgery, so when she speaks of 'openness', she must mean something other than a source of questionable publicity, with the risk that some water damage would require a plumber to descend to the house's lowest rooms.

'Not the usual things?' I ask, clearing my throat again.

'Well, what do you think?' Jutta asks, delaying her answer to make fun of my curiosity a little longer.

'No idea. Swinger clubs, that kind of thing?'

'Rubbish.'

'Well, how should I know? Go on, tell me.'

'We do tantra.'

'Tantra?'

'Yes, tantra.'

Evidently misunderstanding my confusion, Jutta explains that tantra isn't what I think . . .

'I don't think that at all.'

. . . but an ancient Indian system that conceives of body and spirit as a unity.

'I'm even a qualified tantra teacher.'

'And that's okay?'

'Yes, very okay.'

'No, I mean in a small town like this.'

'Well, I don't go shouting it from the rooftops. But it's in my CV.'

'Excuse me, the lady mayor is a tantra teacher?'

'I don't do seminars and stuff like that any more.'

'And people know about it?'

'Whoever wants to know can find out, but it's never been much of an issue here. I mean, I say publicly that people should treat their sexuality as something sacred, that's really important to me. At the national level too.'

Jutta gives a speech of some length on sexuality in the West today, and even if I could probably read something similar in a glossy magazine, I have to admit it captivates me; it genuinely interests me and is also very informative, starting with the fact that an eighth of all websites viewed in Germany . . .

'That's an empirically verified number!'

'What, from the NSA?'

. . . have overt pornographic content. We've completely forgotten that eroticism relies on the secrecy that surrounds it. Fifty years ago, a harmless touch in a novel, even a word like 'thigh', was enough to get young people extremely aroused. By contrast, it's totally normal for today's boys and girls to grow up with obscenity and sexualized ads, and the more shameless the culture industry's gestures are, the greater the resulting de-eroticization. Every young person now has more numerous, more graphic depictions of genitalia and copulation than entire eras ever produced, and children already learn to talk about sexuality in such awful, brutal gutter slang in primary school that one can't start counter-sex education early enough; she's already made suggestions in the party and written to the Minister of Culture. In this moment, she's making her case so plausibly and convincingly that I can genuinely imagine her standing at the lectern. What the kids pick up at YouPorn isn't just vulgar, she says. No, it's wrong, that's just not how sexuality works, it's physically impossible for a woman to have an orgasm that quickly. And for the boys it just lasts a second—how miserable. Like never before in the history of the human race, we're overwhelmed with erotic stimuli, our sex drive is fuelled, but also devalued, commercially exploited and deprived of any higher meaning, so sexual liberation has only led to capitalism treating sexuality like one commodity among many others . . .

'Hey, you're really on fire.'

'You can look it all up.'

. . . names a Frankfurt sexologist . . .

'Highly respected!'

'Never heard of him.'

. . . whose books she recommends. She shudders at the thought of TV shows in which young girls are done up like Barbie dolls . . .

'Oh God, yes . . . '

'I mean, especially as a mother, I see it with my daughter.'

. . . are offered up to the lustful gazes of ever-horny excuses for men, with numbers attached to their half-naked bodies, emaciated from puking bouts, robbed of fertility and thus femininity, turned into children. It's a grave mistake, she says, to confuse eroticism with looseness or to see it as freedom if everything is allowed. Every sensation, every pleasure, and also every freedom and every creative act, at once depend on restraint, restriction, discipline, the same way a river can't flow without its banks, and when she sees young girls tarting themselves up like sex dolls, yes, even her daughter, she starts to sympathize . . .

'Especially as a feminist.'

'Are you a feminist?'

. . . with the people who reject this universal availability, become nuns, wear a headscarf or whatever. Not that she agrees with it, the oppression of women does make her critical of Islam, but she also sees what these young Muslim women are reacting to, and she finds the violation of the body just as terrible, except that it doesn't make her promote prudishness like Islam . . .

'Islam doesn't promote prudishness.'

'Okay, then Islamism.'

. . . but the opposite, namely tantra. It's not just commercial TV, after all; the problem started much earlier, not because of, but nonetheless as a result of the sexual revolution, which she obviously still supports. But people's everyday language is just so wretched.

'Cock, vagina, nipple, scrotum, intercourse, humping—it's awful!'

'Alright, but what else should one say?'

As a counterexample, Jutta names the Indian terms, which genuinely sound like poetry when they're translated . . .

'Is that how ordinary Indians speak?'

'No idea how ordinary Indians speak, that's not the point.'

. . . yet were supposedly already more precise 2,000 years ago than modern science today. Like calling impotence 'erectile dysfunction'.

'It's total nonsense!'

'But the problem can't just be about language.'

The bigger problem, she says, is that people don't talk to each other, they don't say what they want, what turns them on, what they don't like. I have no idea what's out there, she says. There are feeders who fatten their girlfriends, there objectophiles who fall in love with a car, there are cultural sodomites who only live with a dog or a cat—and at the same time, many people don't know how the sexual organs are built, how they work and where they are.

'Take the G-spot, for example,' Jutta exclaims and looks at me expectantly, as if I'm supposed to do something, maybe take the G-spot in my hand or give it to her: 'Does it exist?'

'Yes,' I say, so hesitantly that it sounds like a question. 'Yes?'

'And where is it?'

'It's true,' I agree with an evasive generalization, 'that we don't really know the human body, even though we constantly encounter it in its naked form.'

She asks me if I know that one can cause an orgasm just by stroking someone's hair, that mere stroking can have an effect like electricity, really physically like electricity . . .

'You can measure that!'

'You can measure that?'

 . . . like an electric shock that goes through you as a convulsion. I really should get hold of the new Houellebecq, she urges.

'But that's about something completely different.'

'You haven't even read the book.'

The reader who, like me, always wondered as a child whether heroes don't have to go to the toilet too, won't believe that I can reconstruct the evening with Jutta purely from memory, especially her animated speech. And that reader is right: I will not only condense our conversation, as I have already admitted, moving sentences and entire dialogues from one place to another, misremembering some things or exaggerating other things, putting them in my own words, filling in the gaps in my memory myself—and I'll look things up too.

'You look things up?' I will already be asked by the editor, who is always my first reader.

'Why not?' I will answer, before embarking on a paean to the freedom of the novelist, who can use anything they have on their mind, anything at all: private difficulties, tax demands, bereavements, current reading, fragments of conversations over-heard in the metro, or even headaches, TV news or earworms, because the novel is defined by totality, of which it nonetheless—even in Joyce's hands—falls short. For example, that speech wasn't by Jutta at all. She formulated a similar idea when we went from tantra to modern sexuality, and she ended with tantra, but the part in between was considerably less interesting, really like something from a glossy magazine.

'You're so mean!' Jutta will scold me, as the second reader—or, more realistically, the seventh or eighth—but with affection, the way an older, experienced and more knowing person scolds a friend just to do him the favour of getting worked up.

'That's just my job,' I will say to justify myself, and argue that no reader would be interested in literature if it were as cautious as we humans are in our interactions.

So the speech corresponds to what she was trying to say . . .

'You're so mean!' Jutta will exclaim again, maybe a little more earnestly this time.

'Now wait a minute.'

. . . but is copied word for word, like the love letters that Julien sends to another woman to arouse Mathilde's jealousy.

'You said yourself that I can look it all up in Volkmar Sigusch's book,' I will insist, invoking the highly-respected Frankfurt sexologist.

'But I didn't say anything about tantra,' Volkmar Sigusch will counter when, by coincidence, he reads the novel I am writing.

Jutta asks how we got on to tantra. Somehow by way of Bolivia, I lie, to avoid reminding her that it was because I asked so bluntly about their sex life. Strange that two decades later, she finds it hard to decide if she was happy in Bolivia, yet only mentions situations that made her unhappy.

'So you weren't happy?'

'No, I was happy.'

As I wait for her to continue of her own accord—except she doesn't—I imagine I am watching her call to mind some image or other that she probably won't describe to me, because she finds the situation too unremarkable, nothing one can really talk about, just a kind of feeling, and then keeps returning mentally to the armchair she's sitting in; no, not the armchair—how am I supposed to know all this if she stops talking?—to the study, where her husband is possibly still doing his accounts, back and forth: between the man in Bolivia, whom she'd only known for one or two years, and the man in the study, whom she knows better than she knows anyone else on earth, even better than the children, who are no longer the same at sixteen as they were at eight, and will be different again in another ten years—better than her own parents, half of whose life she only knows from the family album, and these days they only see each other every few weeks at visits, when there's not much chance to talk—the man whose every pore, turn of phrase and habit, whose smell, breath and every skin particle she knows, every orifice, every elevation, every hollow and everything that arouses him, yes, and especially the hair, when mere stroking brings him to climax and he practically goes wild—so sweet!—twitching in her arms, wheezing, surrendering himself, naked, defenceless and joyful, the closest person on earth and yet so foreign to her, like before, when they were arguing about the cereal bowls, not even arguing really— or was it crisp bags?—that's right, the crisp bags, strictly speaking he just articulated his annoyance in the most polite words, no more than that, so foreign in such moments, which aren't moments, they drag on for days and weeks, so proper, polite and distanced that she'd almost like to address him formally, because she can't get inside his feelings and he can't get inside hers, because he locks her out of his thoughts and she locks him out of hers, because he's unhappy and so is she.

'I was happy, but sad too. Or the other way round, no idea.'

One time she came home, late, another day when nothing had worked out—workmen, authorities, errands, she can't remember—then in the evening the parish fair too, where she was selling raffle tickets because, on top of everything else, she wanted to be part of the neighbourhood and not the arrogant foreigner. Her Spanish was almost accent-free now, much better than his, which often aroused laughter when he spoke earnestly to the staff—so German!—but no one at the parish fair was interested in her beyond the obligatory 'How are you? Where are you from? Oh, how exciting!', and certainly no one responded to her attempts to start a conversation about social issues; on the contrary, the women practically fled as soon as Jutta brought up a political subject, and she couldn't speak to the men anyway, who either ignored her, not even greeting her, or paid her inappropriate compliments. No, she couldn't even speak to the priest, who claimed never to have heard of liberation theology, only Christ could offer liberation, so he didn't understand the term. She came home, he had just got back as well, the nanny had long since gone to bed . . .

'Totally crazy! I'm hanging around at this bloody parish fair and selling raffle tickets to the ruling class instead of putting my baby to bed.'

. . . and she found him in the kitchen, where he was just getting a beer out of the fridge and handed her a bottle too, without asking, and it was this feeling, it's bloody awful . . .

'Which Bolivia wasn't at all, it was just tough at the beginning.'

. . . what on earth are we doing here? And me in particular, what am I doing going to this parish fair, although you warned me five times that it would be a complete waste of time; messing around with insurance salesmen who think they can con a foreigner; keep seeing the poverty while I'm at the parish fair, can't get it out of my mind anyway, every time I drive over the bridge and pass the children with tubes of glue held to their noses; and I think to myself, I'm in the wrong film, I'm in the wrong film here in this car, I'm in the wrong film at this parish fair, I'm in the wrong film with this life—but so are you, I see that, it doesn't seem like your day was any better, as tired and strained as you look, with your weary eyes, in this dishonest system you entered for my sake: you're in the wrong film too, in the same wrong film as me. It was just a feeling; they didn't speak, they'd both had enough of 'How are you? Where are you from? Oh, how exciting!', just a feeling, but the same feeling at the same time in one place, she saw that in his weary eyes, just as he saw his own feeling in her eyes . . .

'It was like a vision that whatever happens, the two of us have got each other and the child given to us.'

. . . and then his eyes suddenly lit up . . .

'Really like a vision, that's the only way I can describe it.'

. . . and hers no doubt too, and they held each other, and from one moment to the next that shitty day had become maybe the most beautiful day they experienced during their whole time in Bolivia, although Bolivia would get much better.

'Shall we open another bottle of wine?' asks Jutta, visibly glowing.

'I don't know,' I reply. 'It's already late, isn't it?'

'I'm so churned up inside, I can't sleep now anyway. But maybe you should? Don't you have to get up early tomorrow.'

'Well, who knows when we'll meet again.'

While Jutta gets the wine from the cellar, I go back to the bookshelf. I'm already sketching the novel I'll write in my mind, though the sketch has little in common with what the reader is holding now. Only the starting situation is the same: after reading from a novel about his first love, a novelist is approached by a middle-aged woman, and it's her—'the schoolyard beauty', the heroine of that novel, 30 years after their love, which was probably more significant for him than for her. He invites her to join him for dinner with the organisers, and because they don't get into much of a conversation there, they subsequently go for a stroll through the small town, where she lives with her family. Finally she asks him if he wants to come to her place for a glass of wine. But, as the reader will long have suspected, I have a completely mistaken idea of what follows from this opening, of how the evening, and thus the story, will develop. To be honest, I'm still thinking of an affair, or even more than an affair, that might arise between the novelist and his schoolyard sweetheart, though I don't picture the evening quite as tackily as I did directly after our encounter, with the night at her home or my hotel room, and, with the husband in the study, I realize that I definitely won't be waking up in her arms and sloping off to the station with her after a late breakfast; and with her three children, I certainly don't start wording any phone calls or letters with which we'll stay in touch, our reunion and the love that no longer arises in a second, but lasts forever. God, to think that my day-dreams are nothing but cheap novelettes.

But what I also have in mind, and that counts for more than the plot itself, is the language—or no, not the language, that would already be too much; what I have in mind, or rather in my ear, is the tense of the novel I will write: the present tense, because it more easily absorbs the stream of thought. True, it's also a natural choice to set apart the tense of the meeting that provides the frame story and the memories, which I will keep in the past tense. But at the same time—and this likewise comes to mind while Jutta is getting the second bottle of wine—the present tense allows anticipations of the future in which the novelist will write down his thoughts and reflect on what happens to him in the present. And finally—my sketch won't turn out to be quite as far off the mark after all—I decide that the novel will once again draw on its own story of motifs. I can't choose the mystical literature of the classical Orient again; no, tonight the novelist will open the books on the shelf of his former lover, and thus I begin to leaf through the 20-volume Insel edition of *The Human Comedy* while Jutta is in the cellar, and this reminds me that the French in particular never confused eroticism with permissiveness, which Jutta attacks modern Western society for doing, or saw it as a license to do anything and everything. Maybe she actually got the analogy of the river that can't flow without its banks from Balzac, not tantra.

But *The Human Comedy*, of which I will obtain the Insel edition at a second-hand bookshop in order to read the same translation as Jutta, should evoke on hundreds, if not thousands of pages the arousal that a mere word like 'thigh' can trigger, or, if not a word, then a harmless touch. In *The Girl with the Golden Eyes*, for example, de Marsay, for whom love has become too routine, embarks on increasingly dangerous conquests just so that he can once more feel the thrill of the rare, the forbidden, the mysterious. Time and again, he tries to touch the dress of the seductive, yet strictly guarded Paquita in passing as she walks up and down the promenade with her *dueña* (lady-in-waiting).

> At one point, when he had overtaken the dueña and Paquita in order to find himself beside the Girl with the Golden Eyes when he passed them again, Paquita, no less impatient, took a quick step forward, and de Marsay felt

her squeeze his hand so quickly, but with such passionate meaning, that it was as if he had received an electric shock. In a flash, all the emotions of his youth welled up in his heart.

What she said about the hair sounded rather similar, it also involved electricity. No wonder that I still dream of an affair with Jutta, instead of realizing that the novel I will write is about her marriage.

As I uncork the wine, we return to the subject that interests me as a novelist, but above all as a father. I think of my son, whose snottiness is something like my own personal decline of the West: what does one have to convey to one's children to equip them against the sexualization of the everyday world?

'Not just the children!' Jutta exclaims, switching to politician mode from one sentence to the next. 'All of us! It's our duty, our social duty, to make people understand again that sexuality is something divine.'

'Something divine?'

'You can choose a different word if God doesn't mean anything to you. I just mean the quality that catapults you out of the moment, out of the present, a truly deep, all-encompassing, long-lasting happiness.'

'How long?'

'Not all that long for beginners, but once you're experienced, an orgasm can be drawn out for over an hour, or even longer.'

'An hour?'

'You don't notice it yourself, of course. I mean, you're not timing it. But it can go on for a long time.'

'Longer than an hour?'

'You lose all sense of time. That is, time doesn't exist at all for you any more.'

'So forever.'

'Kind of forever, yes. Or what did you want to say?'

I want to say that Jutta is right, that I more or less understand: in such a state of ecstasy you overcome death, whether it's during sex or something less sensational, like a child immersed in playing, an adult at a concert, whether it's Schubert or Neil Young or whatever, or by the sea, in the mountains, when the beauty of a landscape overwhelms you, or I'm sure you've experienced it under a starry sky: you dissolve, you become one with everything around you, you forget time; and when you step out of time, you've defeated transience for a moment, albeit one that can only be measured from the outside.

'You're not timing it,' I say, adopting Jutta's own formulation.

Then you're eternal, though it's not the composer or the poet or the God who created the music, the poem or nature—no, *you* are eternal, you, the listener, the reader, the observer, while the composer, poet or God, who, in his presumption, might consider himself immortal, will be forgotten after a few decades or centuries, or, at the latest, with the disappearance of humanity, on which even God depends. There is no immortality outside of the world, only inside the world, within us, as it were.

'That's a beautiful thought,' Jutta says, nodding with such exaggerated understanding that I'm not sure if I've expressed myself clearly enough, or if she's just covering up her confusion. 'Our little eternity on earth, a foretaste of paradise.'

'Wow, an hour!' I therefore remark, returning to more concrete matters before the moment of emotion turns into awkwardness because I can't think of a follow-up.

Proust was no more a believer in future paradises than I am, nor in a foretaste. He states this unequivocally on two occasions in *Lost Time*, unless I've missed a passage: once in *Sodom and Gomorrah*, when the novelist doesn't want to see Saint-Loupe's friends again, although they once meant so much to him.

> We desire passionately that there should be another life in which we would be similar to what we are here below. But we do not reflect that, even without waiting for that other life, but in this one, after a few years, we are unfaithful to what we have been, to what we had wanted to remain immortally. Even without supposing that death might modify us more than the changes that occur in the course of a lifetime, if in that other life we were to meet the self that we have been, we would turn away from ourselves as from those people to whom we have been close but whom we have not seen for a long time—those friends of Saint-Loup's, for example, that I was so pleased to find again every evening at the Faisan Doré but whose conversation I would now find simply out of place and an embarrassment. In this respect, and because I preferred not to go and rediscover what had pleased

me there, a walk through Doncières might have seemed to me to prefigure my arrival in paradise. We dream a great deal of paradise, or rather of numerous successive paradises, but they are all, long before we die, paradises lost, in which we would feel lost.

And then there's a passage in *Time Regained*, decades later, that contains almost the same formulation, albeit in relation to the memories evoked in the novelist by something like a madeleine, his childhood cake: 'the only true paradise is a paradise that we have lost.'

Jutta claims there have been people whose orgasms lasted days, and maybe there still are today.

'Days?'

'Yes, days.'

When I counter that this is probably metaphorically intended, the muscles simply aren't physically capable of contracting for that long without spasms, she insists that orgasms lasting days have been documented and one can look it up—not in *Physician's Weekly*, I shouldn't make fun of her, but in texts dating back millennia.

'Seriously, days?'

'Yes, days!'

She's convinced that any person can experience such ecstasy, not for days, not for an hour at the first attempt, but still a fundamentally different reality from the standard in-and-out. One doesn't even need training for it, just mindfulness.

'Mindfulness?'

'Yes, mindfulness, that's all it is really.'

Not everyone who teaches tantra today takes its religious content as seriously as she does, she says. Most of them are spiritually oriented in a more general sense, but she, Jutta, believes she can experience God in sexual rapture. It's a revelation, quite simply, and it's possible for her as a Christian because sexuality is considered divine in all religions. When I note that she previously described Islam as being opposed to sexual pleasure, and that Christianity is hardly famous for its glorification of the carnal, Jutta concedes that she doesn't know enough about Islam—but Christianity definitely isn't un-erotic, just the church, starting with Saint Paul. But Paul is part of Christianity, I remark. Paul is just one possibility of Christianity, she counters, and tantra is simply another.

'And tantra as a possibility . . . '

'Yes?'

' . . . would I find that in Matthew, or rather Luke?'

'What?'

'The steamy bits, I mean.'

'You're such an idiot.'

We both have to laugh now, and the reader shouldn't think of our whole discussion as very serious. The whole time she was talking, she could see the humour in what she was describing to me, and that I was gently teasing her with my questions and interjections, though I was also quite serious, and I'm familiar with the Song of Songs, which is one of the steamiest works of world literature. But even as she giggles, she denies my claim that a Christianity like hers is more of a private religion.

'There's even a work group for Christian tantrists in the party at the national level,' she says, in such a way that I'm not sure if she's joking or if the work group genuinely exists. Well, the reader can Google it if they're interested.

'And the church recognizes it?'

'Well, I don't think they'd give us a stall at the church congress.'

'Would get a bit loud anyway,' I agree with a chuckle.

Without intoxicating substances—the new bottle is already half-empty even though I've stuck to the lemongrass, and she'd already had a few at the restaurant, followed by the joint—the conversation probably wouldn't have developed in such an 'open' way, to use the word with which Jutta praises her marital sex. Or does our early love, however great or slight its importance, have something to do with the fact that talking about her marriage leads her directly to her sex life? No; if anything, it's the special familiarity that one feels almost immediately if one's known someone since childhood or adolescence. Friendships also develop later, deeper friendships, because the interests and concerns people share grow steadier with age; in most cases, we don't have much in common with childhood friends when we see them again after decades. With them it's something different, I think, maybe what amazes us is just the fact that we remain one and the same person, however often the earth has rotated in the meantime: we're still the same, we see each other not only with today's eyes, but also with our youthful eyes. It seems like a dream—no, like a trip, as if that one puff on a joint had worked after all, or as if I were tasting that madeleine both now and in a distant moment, 'so that the past was made to encroach upon the present and make me uncertain about which of the two I was in.'

On the one hand, I'm sitting opposite a woman who's a complete stranger, strictly speaking, who seemingly has nothing in common with the girl who introduced me to love when I was 15; who looks different, speaks differently and has become a different character; who moves differently, has different views, a completely different life, a husband who, one floor above us, may be trying to imagine what I'm like while I try to imagine what he's like; who has three children of whom she hasn't even shown me a photo and a life that I can still hardly believe: a mayor! Someone I wouldn't have recognized unprompted, because that mystified feature, the gap between her teeth, no longer exists; and yet, beneath the present, like a picture under a stencil that doesn't fit, I can still see the girl shining through, speaking to me and looking at me with the same eyes—yes, her eyes really are the same!—who also has the same smile, whose words still have the familiar melody and even the regional colour of our shared background, especially with the 'R', which I also find resisting my efforts to speak High German. And that determination about something she stands for, an opinion or a concern, this passion that she can conjure up out of nowhere, as if she had far too many passions, this compassionate, warm gaze—yes, that's her, the prettiest girl in the schoolyard who turned out to be a squatter, this zeal with which she stands up for what's right, almost takes it over; maybe a do-gooder, as people say dismissively nowadays, but it's a thousand times better than the cynicism other people use to ennoble their own indolence, and she's as convincing as a politician needs to be; beauty too, still beauty, though it's a different kind now, almost under attack, more vulnerable, more exhausted, with cracks like those one finds in early Madonnas, and no doubt her body's not as tempting as it used to be, despite all her efforts—God, when she reads my locker room talk—her skin can't possibly be taut now, her age is simply obvious in her face, and with age, time, and with time, death; and yet still a beauty, still and maybe now even more, because of its transience.

I keep trying to reconcile these two people, the girl and the woman sitting before me, who's fortunately more cheerful again, albeit tipsy too, to say the least, and I make connections, derive this observation from that memory, trace her statements about everything including tantra back to her views at the time, seem to recognize individual movements, gestures, her facial expressions, her choice of words; but I could just as easily be wrong, be imagining it all, I could actually be sitting opposite a stranger, and so could she. Also, she talks openly about her sex life at the national level too.

The question is, to return to the situation in front of the fridge, did her husband have that vision too, or did he just give her a beer? After all, it's the most natural thing in the world, if you're standing in front of the fridge and there's someone behind you, to offer them a beer too. It doesn't even have to be somebody you love; any polite person would hand a mere acquaintance or a guest a beer too, especially so late—why else would one go to the fridge after coming home late than to get a beer, especially if one knows the other person well, if one lives with them, is married to them, and knows that they like to down a beer, a cold beer from the quarter-litre bottles that were already standard in Mediterranean countries 30 years ago—clearly there's no need to ask. Yes, the question is more whether she didn't just imagine that glow in his eyes, if I think of all the spectacular misunderstandings with my own wife that were revealed one by one in our marriage counselling, until, after 20 sessions or thereabouts, we agreed on a divorce; despite our son, whom I kept bringing up as a counterargument, it became so obvious that our marriage had been one great misunderstanding, though our son is anything but a misunderstanding, as even my wife had to admit, despite disagreeing with everything else. But the therapist didn't accept that; instead, she demonstrated—without words, of course; probably no counsellor would tell their clients to their faces that their marriage had failed—with everyday situations like a supper in silence that a quick separation would be best for the child too; that was how disastrous the counselling revealed our marriage to be, a misunderstanding from start to finish, because we'd never spoken to each other, and when we had, we just spoke at cross purposes, as the counsellor showed: my wife had said something I could only take the wrong way, while I'd said something she hadn't understood, luckily hadn't understood, I have to say, otherwise she probably would have wanted a divorce much sooner; though, on the other hand, the continuation of the marriage wasn't ultimately fortunate, as even I had to concede during counselling. God, it shouldn't have taken 20 sessions to get that, it would have been cheaper to read Proust and see how, in love, we often do the opposite of what we feel, such as saying something hurtful in response to a harsh remark, instead of admitting that we're hurt: 'There is nothing like desire for obstructing any resemblance between what one says and what one has on one's mind.' And now Jutta comes along and invokes that one moment—just one, I'd love to ask her, just that one beer thrust silently into her hand during a quarter-century, that's it?— in which they didn't say anything, but she just saw his eyes light up, and he supposedly saw hers do the same, and neither of them spoke, because the vision of their oneness was clear enough without it, so obvious to him too that he didn't say anything and just took her in his arms. And why wouldn't he have embraced her if she was smiling at him, probably already leaning towards him, maybe against him—could he just have leant back and refused the embrace if he had felt like it? Then she would have burst into tears, especially after such a fiasco of a day; or even if she hadn't, it would certainly have guaranteed a crisis. Maybe he just wanted to be left in peace, maybe his thoughts were elsewhere, and he had no choice but to embrace her, which he presumably didn't mind doing; and the glow in his eyes, maybe that was just the lamp in the kitchen, assuming she didn't imagine it altogether. Didn't they at least clink glasses before or after embracing? Now I'd like to know whether he even remembers the situation at the fridge. 'It is the wicked deception of love,' Proust tells us in the third volume of *Lost Time*, which I'm sure Jutta didn't reach,

> that it begins by making us dwell not upon a woman in the outside world but upon a doll inside our head, the only woman who is always available in fact, the only one we shall ever possess, whom the arbitrary nature of memory, almost as absolute as that of the imagination, may have made as different from the real woman as the real Balbec had been from the Balbec I imagined; a

dummy creation which little by little, to our own detriment, we shall force the real woman to resemble.

'But when we make love, he speaks to me. And then I do hear him. Then I do feel him. Then I do breathe him. Then I do see him. Then I grasp him with my hands, with my fingertips, with my knees, my neck, my skin, then I grasp under my skin. His heart's beating as if it were inside me, as if I had two hearts, his and mine. Then I smell him. Then, after so many years, I can tell at once if something's wrong. And he can tell from me. When we make love we become one, or, if we're not one, we notice at once. That's like an electric shock, so clear, when something's wrong, it goes right into your body and really wails inside you. I can't lie to him when we make love, it just doesn't work. And he can't lie either, I know that. Then he doesn't sleep with me, which drives me crazy—not because I'm horny, but because he's evading me, because he's turning me away. Or when he sleeps with me, he doesn't even try to pretend. It hurts much more then, that honesty, that brutal honesty of his, especially when we make love. Then it shifts, it goes totally in the opposite direction. You can't live together if you're only ever honest with each other. But you can make love. Even when it's brutal, it's still beautiful, or no, it's not beautiful, it's—how shall I put it?—it's . . . that we can feel alien to each other, that we know what it feels like not to become one when we make love: doesn't that prove that we can also become one? And do become one sometimes. It's probably no more than that, the fact that this possibility still . . . still exists.'

Aside from one or two childhood memories, by far the most tender scene in the whole of *Lost Time* is the one in which Albertine is sleeping: 'I have spent delightful evenings talking or playing games with Albertine, but I was never so happy as when watching her sleep.' Twice Albertine sleeps, twice for pages; such is the importance for the novelist of the sight that teaches him 'the secret intimacy of pure, unalloyed love'. The novelist does not describe how he sleeps *with* her; this would probably be too much intimacy for him, or perhaps he is reluctant to define the delusions, misunderstandings and missed opportunities that he normally describes so intensely, so meticulously, in the realm of sexuality too, for fear of disenchanting them— reading *Lost Time*, one barely dares to love again anyway.

Or is there some other reason why the novelist always just sits by Albertine's bed, her forehead motionless while the carriages pass noisily in the street, lips closed and breathing reduced to the bare minimum, her eyebrows slightly arched and curved above her eye sockets like a bird's nest, the eyelids lowered just enough to touch each other? Considering the tradition in which Proust stands, I doubt that he omitted their physical union for fear of a scandal, especially considering that the unabashed description of homosexual and sadomasochistic desire would have been more shocking than any conventional eroticism. No, Proust only believes in fulfilment that takes place in the memory or the imagination: 'I already knew several Albertines in one; now I felt I was seeing many more at rest beside me,' he writes, and a little later adds: 'Every time she moved her head she created a new woman, often undreamed of by me.'

The love succeeds, yes, but at the cost of Albertine's individuality; her features are no longer disturbed by pupils, and she takes on a gazeless, almost masklike and thus universal, super- or inhuman beauty. Though not normally prone to any form of sacralization, the novelist at the sleeping Albertine's bedside speaks of the 'truly heavenly' sound of her breathing, the 'pure song of the angels', breaths 'which seemed to be drawn from a hollow reed rather than a human being'; he also mentions her 'folded' hands, and finds her pose 'so naively childish [ . . . ] that, as I looked at her, it was hard not to smile as we do at babies in their innocent gravity and grace.' The lack of 'all knowledge of evil' that he ascribes to Albertine in her sleep, in contrast to the hundreds of pages he devotes to lamenting her deviousness, not only reminds us through association of the absence of sin in biblical paradise; no, the novelist expressly calls this sight 'truly heavenly for me', thus contradicting his own view that paradise can only be found in the past, or at best in listening to music or regarding nature:

> I experienced her sleep with a disinterested, calming love, as I might spend hours listening to the unrolling of the waves. Perhaps it is only people who can make us suffer a great deal who can offer us, in our hours of remission, that same, pacifying calm that nature can give. I did not have to answer her, as I did when we talked, and even had I been able to keep silent, as I did when she was speaking, listening to her did not allow me to enter so deeply into her as I did now. As I went on listening, collecting up from moment to moment the murmur, calming as an imperceptible breeze, of her sweet breath,

a whole physiological existence was laid before me, was
mine [ . . . ].

Although they are supposedly no longer affectionate to each
other, she sometimes, admittedly not often, lies next to her husband in the dark in a way that she didn't 23 or 20 or 15 years ago,
so peacefully, exhausted from the day and without sex: his leg
over her bottom, her hand on the back of his head, their lips close
together or on top of each other, or interlocked like two cogs
standing still for the moment, and the tongues are still playing
with each other or resting too. Then she hears him breathing and
vice versa, that most fundamental of all bodily activities, not only
for humans. Impossible to identify a breathing person purely
from the sound; it is the human being, the creature per se, that
she hears breathing. She notices that her breathing seamlessly
aligns with his, and his with hers, until all the air flows in and out
again in synchronization. She concentrates on his breathing and
assumes he is doing the same, otherwise they couldn't remain in
harmony. Or does that also happen by itself? Yes, it does happen
by itself; she realizes this because her thoughts can wander and
return without any divergence in their breathing. Even when she
lets her thoughts drift deliberately, she still breathes together with
him. Finally, she trusts that they are breathing together and only
pays attention to the air flowing simultaneously through her
body and his, surrendering to the movement, which slows down
because more and more air is flowing in and out, flowing simultaneously into and out of his body and hers, until she wonders if
he is asleep yet—perhaps her last conscious thought—and falls
asleep shortly afterwards.

'It's true, we do argue often,' Jutta mumbles. 'We've broken up so often; but we get back together just as often.'

And of course the children. Proust makes the connection himself when he compares his rapture at Albertine's bedside to the delight of a mother watching her child sleeping peacefully. On Sunday they visited the grandparents together, Jutta's parents in the village near my home town, and their eldest—so it's a son and he's already left home, I remember this time—had come too, all five family members on the motorway; the same discussions for the last 20 years about what to listen to, Jutta's husband always with his rock music, their daughter with earphones secretly inserted, but Jutta's husband notices at once—he's even a fundamentalist with it comes to the car radio; the coalitions that form, the youngest usually on the father's side when the latter suggests an audiobook as a compromise but the daughter always opposed, and their eldest choosing based on whether he wants to emphasize his role as a brother or a fully fledged adult, and Jutta in the passenger seat, either acting as a mediator or sought as a coalition partner. The very notion of no longer arguing in the car, no longer forming majorities, the very notion of scrapping the estate car, as it were, and moving the kids back and forth between the one small car and the other, though everything indicates the journey's been fine until now—according to their own assessment and especially the observations of others: the teachers, relatives and friends who particularly emphasize the self-confidence and groundedness of the children. And they'll start reading again eventually, she sometimes reassures her husband, and even if they don't, they'll have enough other qualities, and her husband says yes, he knows that, and how proud he is of the children and of Jutta as their mother.

'What's to say,' I ask, posing a question I know so well from my own marriage, 'what's to say that the children would be less happy if you separated?'

The marriage she entered into, Jutta continues in a fit of pathos, her voice as firm as for a public declaration, that marriage wasn't sealed at the registry office, not even in church, when she was already pregnant with her second child. She entered into marriage during labour—no, in bed, when she and her husband agreed with a silent glance to make love without contraception.

'That was more beautiful than any celebration,' she says, contradicting her own lament that he had deprived her of a wedding.

Children are the pledge that two lovers make to each other; to her, that's the idea behind the biblical requirement of fidelity and the taboo on divorce. That doesn't mean clinging to a marriage at all costs; it means seeing it with the knowledge of the adults, but from the perspective of the children.

'That still doesn't answer my question,' I insist.

'Yes, I think it does,' Jutta replies. 'If we were arguing all the time, if the children were treated badly, if they didn't feel well at home—okay. But like this?'

'But now the children will be grown soon.'

'Yes, now the children will be grown soon.'

I fear the reader will find the constant literary references somewhat laboured; I already fear this as I sit on Jutta's couch, roughly
sketching the novel I will write. But it's simply the picture that
faces me from my position on the corner sofa: Jutta sitting in the
armchair and the books along the side wall behind her. I listen
to her while looking at the bookshelf, where volumes by
Stendhal, Proust, Balzac, Zola, Flaubert and so on are lined up.
Perhaps I should resist my reflex to intertwine the two, let's say
by keeping the books in mind without constantly quoting from
them. When I write the novel, I'll be aware that the reader will
consider such coincidences fabrications. But then I'll ask whether
your life doesn't equally involve twists of fate that no novelist
would indulge in because they seem too constructed; indeed, perhaps one can measure how true to life a novel is by how
improbable its events are. Events in life aren't logical, and so the
shelf behind Jutta isn't a literary idea but the very reason to tell
the story of our reunion. Jutta's marriage wouldn't ultimately be
interesting enough by itself; then I could have written about my
own, which was just as ordinary. What makes the evening interesting is the coincidence that Jutta is telling me about her
marriage against a backdrop of novels about marriage.

Only through that setting do I realize that adultery is,
outwardly at least, no longer the major event that it was for
Balzac's or Zola's readers, although it has neither become rarer
nor less hurtful to its victims. Nor is physical ecstasy, despite the
sexualization of everyday life that Jutta so passionately opposes,
as dominant now as it was in the literature of the nineteenth and
early twentieth century, where it admittedly appears almost
exclusively outside of marriage. What stands out in our middle-

class marriages is the children. One reads so much about the egotism of Western society, one hears the mantra of self-realization from every direction—and yet most parents only talk about their children; they don't mention themselves when speaking about their families, because the children have become the centre of attention, worry and reflection. Just take *Madame Bovary*, I think to myself, because I want to incorporate the bookshelf quite frequently into the novel I will write: Berthe, the daughter, barely appears, and does not seem to interest either the adulteress or Monsieur Bovary especially. At most, the cuckold uses the daughter in order not to lose Emma, appealing to her maternal feelings, which are so underdeveloped that the daughter's feelings have long since withered too: when Madame kills herself, Berthe is simply told that her mother has gone away and will bring back some toys. 'Berthe mentioned her again several times; then, eventually, forgot about her.'

I've always asked myself what anyone could find appealing about Emma—'I'll be in love with Emma Bovary until my dying day,' Mario Vargas Llosa gushed, and one finds a plethora of similar comments in literature—a self-centred, superficial, inconsiderate creature that Flaubert precisely *didn't* conceive as a model or object of longing: 'a woman of false poetry and false emotions', he called her in a letter. On top of that, she's such an uncaring mother that Monsieur Bovary doesn't feel any need to compensate for his daughter's pain with additional affection; he initially clings to Berthe, but in the way one clings to a souvenir that stands for a precious memory, before he loses interest. He's not much of a support for his daughter either, practically leaves her to her own devices, doesn't even talk to her and doesn't show the slightest ambition to preserve his own economic existence, which Berthe's future naturally depends on too. He recklessly squanders her inheritance and keeps wallowing in his misery: after Flaubert describes at length how Monsieur Bovary no longer goes out, no longer receives guests and even refuses to see to his patients, instead gazing timidly out of the window all day with his long beard and dirty clothes or walking up and down the garden crying, he flatly states that Berthe must accompany her father to the cemetery every afternoon. 'They used to come back at nightfall, when the only light to be seen was in Binet's attic window.' That's the only thing Monsieur Bovary does with his daughter: force her to accompany him to the grave of his wife, who also happened to be her mother. His responsibility for his daughter doesn't keep him alive any more than it did Madame Bovary. When little Berthe calls him to supper, he 'had his head back against the wall, his eyes closed, his mouth open, and in his hand was a tress of long black hair'—still the hair of his long-deceased wife.

> 'Come on, daddy!' she said. And, thinking that he was only playing, she gave him a gentle push. He fell to the ground. He was dead.

The way Monsieur and Madame Bovary treat their daughter is scandalous, a level of neglect and disregard that would lead to intervention by child protection services and judges nowadays—this is barely mentioned in passing, being of little interest to the reader. Berthe is passed on to her grandmother, who soon also dies, then an aunt takes her in but sends her to a cotton mill; for young girls in nineteenth-century France, this was a direct route to prostitution. Yet Flaubert is no more interested in a literary elaboration on Berthe's misfortune than her parents had been interested in her life. How ironic that today's ostensibly godless society seems to follow Jutta's prescription, which is a secularized form of the Christian one: that children are the purpose of the marriage.

As a result, the difficulties I have with my son make it almost unbearable to hear other parents raving about their children with all the sentimentality of lovers. Jutta just keeps going. Who cares that her eldest is involved with Blockupy because he's extremely interested in financial flow, that her daughter will no doubt shake off her crazy ideas about becoming a model and that her youngest has already read *The Trial*? That's exactly what characterizes parental love: it can make any lout adorable, any frump enchanting and any outrage forgivable. Proust's friends couldn't find anything appealing about Albertine after he had spent hundreds of pages describing her as the ultimate ideal, and I feel myself re-enacting this as grotesque as Jutta repeatedly swipes her smartphone to display her loved ones to me from every angle. 'I was not unduly distressed,' the novelist shrugs. 'Let us leave pretty women to men with no imagination.' No doting mother, fledgling father or youthful lover can react so calmly. No doubt I would be allowed to make fun of her husband, but Jutta doesn't show him to me, although I'm far more interested in him. I dread to think what would happen if I admitted that her children strike me as fairly ordinary. She may be scared by her daughter's modelling craze, for example, but I can only treat it as a joke, for what I see on the screen is a chubby little girl—with a brace, no less. What a miracle of the imagination it is to see her daughter as a beauty; these are the miracles that love works.

If one of Jutta's children were incurably ill, addicted to drugs or the victim of an accident, of course I would take notice, share her worries and empathize sincerely. But children who grow up healthy and sheltered, whatever headaches they cause their parents here and there, are all the same to an outsider. Tolstoy's opening statement in *Anna Karenina* that all happy marriages are similar, while each unhappy marriage is unhappy in its own particular way, would now apply first of all to the children. And that's ultimately the direction of Jutta's argumentation: she adduces the children to defend her marriage. The books behind her would never have resorted to that.

'But that's not really true,' Jutta insists, and refers of her own accord—no, no, no, I'm not making it up, this is genuinely like a film or a cheap novel, how will I ever make it plausible to the reader?—she refers of her own accord, although she has no idea of the sketch in my head, to Balzac's *The Memoirs of Two Young Wives*. 'Do you know it?'

I don't, as it happens; I've never been a Balzac reader until now, but I will buy the book as soon as I get home, and find that he already encapsulated the dilemma of marriage today. One only has to bring the two memoirs together, viewing the account of a marriage of love and the account of a marriage of convenience as belonging together, like two acts of the same play, and one finds a shockingly accurate description of what, almost 200 years later, often comes close to crushing us in marriage: the expectation that infatuation and marriage genuinely belong together, and that romantic feelings have to assert themselves in everyday coexistence. Jutta doesn't adduce Balzac to speak of marriage, however, but about children, which certainly can be the reason and purpose of a family in French literature.

> One does not love in the same way at every moment; love does not embroider the fabric of life with inevitably glowing flowers. Love can and must end, but motherhood need fear no decline, it grows in concert with the child's needs, it develops along with him. Is it not all at once a passion, a need, an emotion, a duty, a necessity, happiness itself? Yes, darling, there is the life that is women's alone. In it our thirst for devotion is sated; in it we find none of the turmoils of jealousy. For us, then, it is perhaps the only point at which Nature and Society coincide.

Last summer her daughter didn't come home one night, Friday night, her phone was switched off or didn't have any reception. All Jutta and her husband knew was that she'd planned to go to friends, because normally she's never more than 10 or 15 minutes late, or calls if she'll be later than that. She understands that reliability is the currency with which she can stay out longer and stop her parents from asking where, what for and with whom. There aren't many places to go out in this little town anyway— an ice cream parlour, a hookah lounge, the small pedestrian zone or, in the summer, the barbecue area or the minigolf course. Had someone taken their daughter to the next big city, which is almost an hour's drive away? It turned out to be more harmless, she'd simply got totally drunk for the first time and fallen asleep on the swimming pool lawn, but the way Jutta and her husband communicated almost wordlessly—she rang all her daughter's friends while he drove around town—the way the parents kept in touch by phone and decided purely by telepathy to inform the police, the way they both kept calm when the police appeared in their living room barely five minutes later, each careful not to infect the other with their own distress and excitement, which were no use to anyone, the way their words complemented each other precisely when they spoke to the police and later the detective inspector, without one ever interrupting the other—they weren't just symbiotic as parents then, but as lovers too.

By the time they were released from their ordeal around six in the morning—that late!—by the news that a patrol car had found their daughter, who had finally woken up and climbed over the swimming pool fence, they had got through the most terrible night of their lives together, and could only have got through it together; this made their subsequent embrace all the more tender. Simply knowing that the night was just as awful for the other person made the bond between them visible. Yes, that fear for their daughter was so much more terrifying than any conceivable marital dispute including separation, any personal hardship or the death of their parents, say, which will inevitably happen, whereas the death of their own child, which Jutta and her husband had imagined without speaking about it, is the ultimate unforeseen and insurmountable event—that night was so much more terrifying, and yet also a oneness that was further reaching, stronger and more intensely emotional than any physical entwinement. Even the detective inspector praised Jutta and her husband in parting, saying he'd never experienced such impressive, well-functioning parents in his whole career . . .

'I mean, isn't that worth something?' asks Jutta, wiping the tears from her face.

'Yes,' I reply, unsure if I should go over to her armchair and hug her at the very moment she's defending her marriage. 'That *is* worth something.'

What remained of that night, however, was not the symbiosis they achieved in more ways than just sexually. What remained was the abyss that opened up beneath them, because they secretly feared their daughter had been raped, however often the police offers reassured the parents and the parents reassured each other—but violent crimes happen more often in the country than the city, proportionally speaking, and the use of knockout drops to make young girls defenceless is certainly a real phenomenon in her area, one the inspector would certainly not deny, and there had been warnings about them at parents' evenings—an abyss also for their marriage, which would have been shattered by such a disaster.

'How do you know that?' I ask.

No, one can't know something like that. Nonetheless, during that whole night, when she was trembling, praying and, most of all, pulling herself together, she had the strong and incessant feeling that her marriage wouldn't last another day if a misfortune had befallen their daughter; that the misfortune, instead of binding them closer together like the worrying that preceded it, would immediately tear them apart. Just the thought of the accusations, which he wouldn't even have to utter for her to shriek with rage: that she allowed the children too much, that she doesn't keep an eye on them, that what she passed off as liberal parenting was really just laziness, all the broken records she had heard so often, which he would never fall back on after such a calamity, he's not that insensitive—which, she phrases more carefully, he probably wouldn't fall back on, wouldn't have to fall back on; the mere memory is enough, because those broken records push her buttons, rightly or wrongly. After all, he wouldn't play them if they didn't.

An abyss beneath her existence as a whole. 'I am just back from hell,' Renée writes to Louise, referring neither to a marital dispute, personal hardship or the death of her parents. By comparison, none of that matches what she calls hell: 'not five days but five centuries of pain'. She is referring to her son's life-threatening illness. 'There were moments when I counted you lucky for not having children—you see how far I was from my right mind!' Emotional descriptions always seem rather over the top in old novels, with constant prostrations, perennial tears, eternal vows and slavish subjection; but what Renée laments would be felt just as dramatically by any contemporary mother fearing for her child today: the horror that fills her soul at the mere thought of such a catastrophe, when the mother feels all the bonds that tie the child to her quaking heart.

> Dear God! With what horrible pains you attach the child to his mother! What nails you drive into our hearts to hold him in place! Was I then not yet mother enough, I who wept with joy on seeing that child's first steps, on hearing him stammer out his first words? I who study

him for hours at a time so as to properly perform my duties and inflict these terrors, these horrible visions, on one who makes an idol of her child?

Balzac dedicated *The Memoirs of Two Young Wives* to his friend George Sand, the icon of equal rights. This suggests that his sympathies lay with Louise, who wants to relish life, instead of seeing her destiny in a marriage of convenience like Renée. 'You marry and I love!' Louise says, putting her attitude in a nutshell, and practically has a fit when she hears of Renée's pregnancy: 'I already hate your future children; they will be ill-begotten. Everything is planned out in your life: you will have no cause for fear, for hope, for suffering.' And indeed, Renée openly admits that she does not love her husband 'with the love that makes the heart beat faster at the sound of a footstep, that sends a thrill through the soul on hearing a single word or feeling the embrace of an ardent gaze'. Even when she thinks she is writing positively about her feelings, she proves the opposite: 'but neither does he displease me.' She justifies her decision to marry with such a lack of illusions that a modern reader might shiver just like her friend Louise; she speaks of 'duty', of 'sacrifice', of 'the terrible deed that changes a girl to a wife and a lover to a husband', and her later description of married life—she and her husband go to bed at nine every evening and rise at daybreak, the meals are served with dreary punctuality, the days pass without the slightest incident—is as monotonous as life in the convent from which both women have fled: 'Once I was a living being, and now I am a thing!' For Renée, happiness is not her own pleasure but her husband's happiness: 'Louis is so contented that in the end his joy warmed my own soul.'

How different is Louise: early on, she realizes the ideal of emancipation that Jutta's generation was still fighting for a 150 years later—'I think women are worth much more than men'—strives for self-realization and insists on sexual autonomy. She expects her future husband to prove his love in life-threatening ways, and is ecstatic when she feels truly wanted. 'Your marriage is a purely social affair, mine nothing more than the fullest fruition of love: two worlds that can no more understand each other than the finite can understand the infinite,' she writes to Renée.

> You are on earth, and I in the heavens! You are in the
> realm of the human, and I of the divine. I reign by love,
> and you reign by calculation and duty. I am so high up
> that I would break into a thousand pieces should I ever
> fall. But here I must say no more, for I blush to tell you
> of all the wonder, the richness, the fresh, glowing joys
> of such a springtime of love.

It seems clear where our sympathies lie. But it's not so simple for Jutta. When the novel was published between November 1841 and January 1842 as a feature in the newspaper *La Presse*, a preliminary note articulated Balzac's intention: 'It is an obvious rejection of all new theories about the independence of women, and a work written primarily for a moral purpose.'

Because Renée's absolute love for her children is moving, and it is all the more moving because the novel begins with a description of parental indifference that was evidently considered normal in the mid-nineteenth century. Louise, who, like Renée, was locked up in a convent at the age of nine and not visited once after that, describes in her first letter how she returned to her parents' house as an 18-year-old. The fact that she has to wait for her mother even to greet her in her rooms, and that hours pass before her father makes the effort to see her, is not even the worst thing about her return; for this would simply make them neglectful parents of the kind that there have always been. What's shocking is the self-evidently natural way in which the parents disregard their daughter and the gratitude, even enthusiasm that Louise feels at the little attention she ultimately receives:

> My mother was perfectly gracious: she expressed no false tenderness, but neither was she cold; she neither treated me as a stranger nor clasped me to her bosom like a beloved daughter. She greeted me as if we had seen each other only the day before, like the kindest, most sincere friend; she spoke to me woman to woman, and first of all gave me a kiss on the forehead.

After nine years, all she gives her own daughter when she first sees her is a kiss on the forehead! Balzac makes it clear from the start that the coldness of the parents is simply the flipside of the self-realization he will portray in such radiant colours with Louise; for their daughter was simply bothersome, no more than that, so her parents bundled her off to a convent so that her father can devote himself to his career as a diplomat and her mother to her lovers, and both of them together—with a very open approach—to the Paris salons. And now that the daughter has claimed the freedom to flee from the convent, she is simply received cheerfully because her parents afford her the same selfishness on which they pride themselves: 'At your age, I would have felt just as you do,' says her mother, like a forgiving grandmother, accepting that her daughter has thwarted her plans. As a result, Louise praises her mother to the skies and takes her as an example: 'Several times I kissed her hands, telling her I was overjoyed that she was treating me as she was, that I felt at home here; I even confided to her that I was secretly terrified.' Finally, the mother even addresses her daughter with the informal *tu*.

But Jutta is completely different from Louise at first glance, and not only in her relationship with the children. She doesn't at all, or at least not primarily, strive to taste life in its full richness and intensity, to have the strongest, most fulfilling experiences possible, which is still an ideal today if the glossy magazines are to be believed; she doesn't base her relationships on her own needs at all, as a degenerated psychology tries to fool its consumers into thinking, and always sees her own welfare in connection with that of her family, not seeking fulfilment in erotic love alone. As a squatter, at the age of 19, she was already standing up for causes that weren't individual; she studied medicine for the reason— not only a declared reason, but also one she was subjectively serious about—of helping those in need, and moved to Latin America to immerse herself in that new environment to put her commitment into practice, to the point of exasperation. Not to mention the childcare or the separate rubbish bins that she managed to get introduced as a mere local councillor! One doesn't have to consider sensor-controlled traffic lights a breakthrough in the history of civilization, or a second grass football pitch relevant to humanity. But, to adopt the formulation that

Jutta tearfully applied to her marriage: isn't it worth something that so many commuters can sleep a few minutes longer now, that so many children can hug their parents a few minutes sooner every afternoon, and that emissions have been measurably reduced on the town's outskirts? Isn't it worth something that asylum seekers who waste away in hostels elsewhere contribute to the championships in Jutta's town? (And no one suspects that half a year later, mayors all over Germany would be standing at train stations to welcome the new arrivals.)

I expect Jutta would counter self-critically that intelligent traffic routing affirms the system that produces so much car traffic, that she helps a few refugees, but doesn't do anything about the causes of flight, which she certainly still sees in imperialism, or whatever she calls the hegemonic ambitions of the Western empire these days (Toni Negri is also on the shelf), from the wars over resources in the Middle East to mines with rare-earth elements or land grabs in India by multinational corporations and the Chinese slave labour that went into producing the smartphone on the coffee table. She would admit that her local politics, for all the appeals or even resolutions at the regional convention, or a synod that she may have initiated herself, follows the ideology of economic growth that declares modesty a dirty word, and would be outraged that a neighbourhood fair to which a happy few asylum seekers are invited ultimately only helps to conceal the fact that Europe's isolationist policies (this is the state of things today, sitting in Jutta's living room, but it will probably be the same tomorrow) have never been so murderous. She would point out that she wouldn't be nominated if she advocated open borders, rather than legalizing cannabis, at the national level—or even just higher fuel prices. And woe to anyone who's serious about eliminating hunger in the world, who speaks of justice as a politician. Town twinning is as far as one can go with international solidarity in an election manifesto. Nonetheless, I would still admire her insight, which is so far ahead of my own when I imagine, or perhaps only give the impression during readings at community centres, that I'm ethically consistent. That's what I'd reply if Jutta were dissatisfied with herself, and perhaps I'd also read to her from the little white book that used to be a bible for me. As if I did anything different from local politics; my readership is no bigger than the town she's the mayor of. Her husband at least tries to live by his convictions to some extent, Jutta says. She admires him for his rigour, which repeatedly leads to arguments—or not even to arguments any more.

But Jutta, like all of us, wanted to love like Louise, who flirts with her tutor, who is not especially attractive and is therefore considered unsuitable by society, but is all the more noble-minded and hot-blooded for it; she meets him at night, at the risk of death, and finally marries him in defiance of all conventions. 'Felipe is an angel,' she gushes, floating above the clouds; it has already been eight months since the wedding.

> I can think out loud with him. I mean no rhetorical flourish when I say that he is another me. He is finer than words can say: he grows more fondly attached to what he possesses, and in his happiness discovers ever new reasons to love. To him I am the finest part of himself. I can see it: years of marriage, far from altering the object

of his passions, will heighten his faith, will develop new sensibilities, and will strengthen our union. What a happy delirium!

Even her mother envies her daughter for 'superbly' achieving what was so rare then, but is considered obligatory now: turning one's lover into a husband. And she repeats it! After being widowed, she loses her heart to an equally passionate, even poorer man and, against all reason, marries out of love once again, this time even in secret: 'Our thoughts are the reverberation of the same thunderclap,' the lover tells a friend whom he needs for the ceremony as a witness. 'Our path has been strewn with the flowers of tender imaginings. Each hour brought its own wealth, and when we parted, it was to put our thoughts in verse.' To be undisturbed by gossip, and because the Parisian delights mean nothing alongside their *amour fou*, the couple moves to the country, where they live purely on love and bread, as it were. Two years later, Louise describes her still-wonderful everyday life, sleeps late and has breakfast in bed; then it is already midday, and because it is hot, the lovers treat themselves to a little siesta.

> Then Gaston wishes to look at me, and he gazes on my face as though it were a picture, losing himself in this contemplation, which, as you may suppose, is not one-sided. Tears rise to the eyes of both as we think of our love and tremble.

I know such an idyll is almost comical to read, but wouldn't a never-ending honeymoon be the purest form of the love we've all imagined, no doubt Jutta too, albeit not with me? Admittedly, such devotion leaves no room for motherly love, otherwise the lovers would have to get up at seven in the morning instead of living for the moment, would have to earn money, eat on time— in short, lead a bourgeois life, and would probably be too tired even to have sex on a regular basis; and when they did, it would be so quietly that they didn't wake anyone, unless they expanded the basement to harbour racks, instruments of torture and such like, so that they could still feel the thrill of the unusual, the forbidden, the secretive. Children, despite being the natural or—in religious terms—divinely ordained result of erotic love, stand in very clear opposition to that. Anthropologically, crisis is preordained after marrying out of love. Hence Louise asks whether Renée would look after her child if she involuntarily became pregnant. In practice, then, 'the great lady's selfishness' that Renée sees hidden beneath the flowers of Louise's spring of love means that Louise would shunt off her children just as she herself was shunted off.

That's what we want, the glossy magazines have been telling us since the time of Proust, whom evidently no one has read, or if so, then not even the greatest novelist achieved much: to become parents while remaining lovers, to be Louise and Renée at once. I am not saying there can only be the one or the other; but the one takes away for the other, and I cannot make out any rule determining which takes from which, when it takes or how much it takes. Jutta, who began to love as Louise, now identifies more with Renée. And indeed, Balzac's mastery lies in letting us watch and feel how the woman who lusts for life, who corresponds to our modern ideal in her independence and courage, simultaneously has a very dark and selfish side, while the bourgeois conformist gradually comes into her own. 'What would you have? Everyday life cannot be cast in heroic mould,' Renée initially writes to Louise, and we are likely curl our lips in disdain at so much docility: 'I can see no opening left for suffering, and I see a great deal of good to be done.' Later we read that Louise, like an addict, craves ever new amorous thrills. Whereas Renée, contrary to all modern psychological advice, sees love as maximum self-sacrifice, Louise's life amounts with maximum narcissism to the wish to be loved. Accordingly, Renée frankly reproaches her: 'You do not love him.' Her verdict: 'Now, as the result of a careful diagnosis of your case, I can say with confidence, this is not love.' Louise, she argues, will never see Felipe as a husband, only a lover with whom she can play as she likes, and it will take at most two years for her to grow sick of her own adoration and despise him for loving her too much: 'you love in Felipe not your husband, but yourself.'

And indeed, as in today's marriages, where Mum becomes a ruler in leather and a naked Dad gives a paw, Louise forces her husband into one humiliation after another. He is her slave, so she can demand anything of him, Felipe grants, as if plagiarizing *Fifty Shades of Grey*—when it's actually the other way around, and the porn industry is just imitating the old novels: 'I have given myself to you absolutely and for the mere joy of giving, for a single glance of your eye.' But Louise scolds him, for his letters still show semblances of spiritual freedom and a clear will of his own: 'This is not the attitude of a true believer, always prostrate before his divinity.' In response, he thanks his mistress with ostentatious masochism for her anger, indeed a jealousy 'like the God of Israel', which fills him with happiness: 'Be jealous of your servant, Louise, I beg of you; the harder you strike, the more contrite will he be and kiss the rod, in all submission, which proves that he is not indifferent to you.' She sets him impossible, even inhuman tasks that put his life in danger; she gives him her hand through the window, which he can only kiss by scaling the high walls in the dark and almost falling. 'But all this is nothing; Christians suffer the horrible pangs of martyrdom in the hope of heaven,' Louise writes coldly to Renée, even boasting of her sadism. And it is no mere rhetoric, these are not simple tests of love like those in *One Thousand and One Nights*; the spiritual violence Louise does to Felipe ruins him physically. 'The exactions, the preposterous jealousy, the nagging unrest of my passion wore him to death,' Louise ruefully admits—only to fall in love anew and equally selfishly soon after Felipe's death.

Renée is unconvinced, and accuses Louise of a heartless egotism that the poetry of the heart simply conceals:

> How noble was the reply of the Duchesse de Sully, the wife of the great Sully, to someone who remarked that her husband, for all his grave exterior, did not scruple to keep a mistress. 'What of that?' she said. 'I represent the honour of the house, and should decline to play the part of a courtesan there.'

As I said, I'll only read *The Memoirs of Two Young Wives* afterwards, and for now only become acquainted with the witty remark from the Duchess of Sully, which Jutta falsely attributes to Renée.

'But it's exactly the other way round with you,' I counter.

Because Jutta doesn't understand the connection, I point out that for Renée, marriage and sex have nothing to do with each other; Jutta, on the other hand, thinks the sex is the only stable thing about her marriage.

'Not the only thing,' she contradicts.

'Alright, obviously the children are a factor too, sure.'

'Not just the children either.'

'I'm sure that's true. I just meant that you have sex, they don't.'

'But that's not the point here. I meant something else.'

Unfortunately I no longer have any idea of what Jutta meant, and what we were talking about earlier, and I can't reconstruct it in the novel that I'll write—or rather, obviously I could, I could look at all the motifs from every side, touch up my experience after the event and polish our words beyond recognition, but then the novel would be untruthful unless it also gave some expression of the memory lapses, sudden leaps and digressions— an expression, I repeat, not necessarily the lapses, leaps and digressions themselves. Didn't Jutta mention that *The Memoirs of Two Young Wives* is one of her favourite books? Yes, but I just can't recall in what context she quoted the remark, which isn't really as original as all that. God, almost four in the morning. Before Jutta reveals the ominous context to me, I ask something I'm genuinely interested to find out:

'What made you take up tantra?'

To save those readers whose ignorance equals my own a trip to Google, I'll copy and paste Wikipedia into the novel I'll write:

> Tantra (Sanskrit for 'loom, weave, system') is a direction within Indian philosophy and religion that initially developed as an esoteric form of Hinduism and later Buddhism within the northern Mahayana tradition. The origins of tantra go back to the 2nd century CE, but the doctrine did not develop in its complete form until at least the 7th or 8th century.
>
> [ ... ]
>
> The word *tantra* is sometimes traced to the Sanskrit root *tan*, 'expand'. Thus tantrism also refers to all-encompassing knowledge or an expansion of knowledge.
>
> [ ... ]
>
> Tantrism emphasises the identical nature of the absolute and the phenomenal world. The aim of tantrism is to become one with the absolute and gain knowledge of the highest reality. As it is assumed that this reality is of an energetic nature, and that microcosm and macrocosm are interwoven, tantrism performs outward acts as a mirror of inner psychic states. As spirit and matter are not considered entirely separate, Hindu tantrism affirms earthly life and uses psycho-experimental techniques of self-realisation and experience of the world and life, whose elements are meant to be experiences as positive dimensions in which the absolute reveals itself.

[ ... ]

In the Western world, tantrism became increasingly known from the early 20th century on, albeit usually reduced to sexual aspects, which are by no means central in classical tantra. Today, tantra is usually offered in the West as neotantra, where the Hindu and/or Buddhist content is treated as secondary to an optimisation of orgasm ability and a striving for sexual-spiritual wellness.

It's probably a good thing, I will think to myself when I write the novel, that I know so little and consider myself too cultivated to grab the smartphone on the coffee table for a quick Google. As a result, I don't question the identical nature of the absolute and the phenomenal world that Jutta wants to experience in sexual fulfilment, this complete oneness not only with the lover, which doesn't even exist in this form, because love—if I understand Jutta correctly—isn't 'made' in the conventional sense, and I probably have to think of the ritual more as a massage: this oneness with everything around her.

It's about breath, says Jutta, breath is the most important thing, over a very long space of time in which your senses are stimulating one by one, starting with your hearing, then your sense of smell, your eyes, the nerves along your skin—breathing evenly and naturally so that the air goes all the way to your fingers, down your legs to the tips of your toes, flows deep into your stomach and down your back, and fills your skull too, before your body's even been touched. You just lie there naked, eyes closed, nonetheless sensing your surroundings, the shifts of light and dark; you feel every unevenness in the mattress, every hint of discomfort in one place or another along your back as well, that's part of it and goes away by itself if you gradually dissolve in perception (like the Chinese painter who steps into his own painting, that's how I imagine it). The ceiling, the floor and the walls almost disappear, leaving you ultimately surrounded not by a room but the universe, and instead of lying heavily on a mattress you feel weightless (wasn't there something about a flying yogi too?), listen to the music (probably best if I don't ask which), smell the incense (still joss sticks 30 years later!) and soon the oil that's being heated for you—and breathe.

Without doing anything, you notice how the volume of breath constantly increases, how when you inhale, the pleasantly cool air fills you so much more than you ever thought possible, and leaves your body incredibly empty when you exhale—this constant alternation between a confusing, barely tangible and yet arousing fullness, and an emptiness that draws you in like death or the void. With enough practice, when the other person finally bends over you, it's enough for their breath to touch you anywhere, it could be your belly or your shoulder or your own half-open mouth, mingling with your own breath, and the first tremor will go through you from head to toe, you'll contort your limbs as if you're having a seizure and moan with pleasure. And that's just the beginning. A single feather that might stroke your body next, like a slightly stronger breeze, or water dripping on you at regular intervals, from your forehead to the chest, past the sexual organs and down your legs to your toes, already puts you in a state of rapture where you can't tell up from down any more. It's generally the case that the more experienced one is, the more well-founded one's knowledge of the energy gates in the body and the deeper one's religious insight, the less one needs to be touched. You're so awake, but without thinking, so present in yourself, that your spirit reacts to mere signs. In the end it's all within oneself anyway, and we only need the other person to find ourselves within ourselves.

The reader will assume that I copied this from a textbook again to describe the process that Jutta meant, but expressed in more basic words. Far from it! I will actually purchase a few of the titles at Amazon with high rankings, higher than any of my own books have reached, but what one finds there reads far more mechanically than Jutta's words. Though they present themselves as Indian religiousness, the handbooks deal mostly with moves and positions that are richly illustrated, maybe with a few breathing commands directly before orgasm. Jutta, on the other hand, describes the ritual so intensely and so vividly, even without any illustrations, that merely listening already arouses me, while reading up on it, especially looking at the photos, has a rather sobering effect. That's why I'll put the handbooks back on the shelf when I write the novel, and just rely on my memory, which is unfortunately no longer in receptive mode at four in the morning. Later still, when she reads the first draft, Jutta will point out that I've got all sorts of things mixed up and have a very imprecise memory, when I'm not just making it up. Yet she won't say it angrily, but with the very same mocking tone that already enchanted me 30 years ago, though it also bothered me—it bothered me because there was something know-it-all and artificially grown up about it, and enchanted me because there was forgiveness and laughter in it.

'Do what you want,' she said, giving me carte blanche. 'Just as long as you don't call me Jutta again.'

'Vinteuil doesn't sound much better,' I will reply, referring to the most famous pseudonym from *In Search of Lost Time*, so that she'll let me use her name. Unfortunately, my intellectual ostentation doesn't work on her.

Although he barely writes about fulfilment, because longing leads directly to melancholy, I'll stumble on a passage in Proust that illuminates Jutta's description more than any neotantric handbook—specifically her point that the greater one's experience and the deeper one's insight, the less one needs to be touched. That's right: it's still the business with the hair that I can't get out of my head, the idea that the slightest stimulation of the scalp can be enough to make your spirit explode. I just wonder if that's possible: fulfilment. In Proust, longing doesn't turn into melancholy *despite* its fulfilment, but *because of* it: for me, the fact that no reality can live up to what a lover promises himself was never an argument against reality, but for love. Only artistic beauty multiplies with experience, Proust says. The beauty of a woman, however, is due mostly to the imagination of the observer, who, if anything, should be protected from experience—that is, from overly precise and repeated viewing—if it is to remain fully intact.

Haven't we all experienced how the glances that tempt us most and hold the greatest mystery are the most fleeting ones? Proust veritably invokes this imprecise and inadequate glance:

Nightfall and a coach travelling fast, in the country or in town, are all that any female torso requires, mutilated like an ancient marble by our speeding departure and the concealing dusk, standing at a road-junction and in every lighted shop, shooting the arrows of Beauty at our heart, and making us wonder at times whether Beauty in this world is ever anything other than the makeweight which our imagination, overwrought by regret, adds to a fragmentary and fleeting passer-by.

And Proust is right, of course, that we are better off not alighting to approach the woman, for as little as an unevenness in her skin or even a curious accent would rid us of all illusions; and even if we did find the face flawless, it would never again be as mysterious and intangible and supernatural as in our imagination. Beauty would cross over into our own reality and inevitably—in the most favourable case, that is, if the woman returned our sympathy—become mundane. How different it is with artistic beauty, like poetry or *Lost Time* itself!

It often happens, he tells us, that when listening to a somewhat complex piece of music for the first time, one doesn't hear anything, or at least not what really matters. One certainly hears it, but doesn't retain it. What's missing after the first listen isn't understanding but memory. Compared to the multiplicity of things with which they are confronted, our powers of memory are as feeble and limited as the memory of a childish old man who forgets a minute later what one has just said to him. The memory is incapable of supplying us with a mental reproduction of such diverse impressions on the spot. But this image gradually forms, and with works one has heard two or three times, it is like with the student who reads a lesson several times before sleep without retaining it, yet recites it from memory the next morning. 'Not only does one not immediately discern a work of rare quality; but even within such a work, as happened to me with the Vinteuil sonata, it is always the least precious parts that one notices first.'

If I understand Proust correctly—or the way I want to understand him, I admit—then pleasure consists in recognizing something familiar, and the more delicate, the more subtle what we remember is, the greater and more emphatic the fulfilment will be. Compared to the celebration of sensuality Jutta describes, ordinary sex would probably be like a pop song compared to a sonata; or, if one imagines it without the foreplay after a few years of marriage, like a party hit compared to a symphony. In private, I might think that a party hit can also have its merits, especially in one's youth; but for anyone who, like Jutta, has learnt to grasp love as a work of art, the brute pounding one can watch on an eighth of all websites viewed in Germany must seem repugnant. An orgasm triggered by the mere stroking of the hair takes place, must take place in the infinity of the imagination, at most activated, but not created by the external stimulus—I don't really know if it's the tantric view, but certainly from a mystical perspective, beauty within ourselves is always greater because God is within ourselves.

Nonetheless, I do wonder if Proust is right when he sees nothing intermediate between longing and melancholy:

Because it was only in successive stages that I could love what the sonata brought to me, I was never able to possess it in its entirety—it was an image of life. But the great works of art are also less of a disappointment than life, in that their best parts do not come first. In the Vinteuil sonata, the beauties one discovers soonest are also those which pall soonest, a double effect with a single cause: they are the parts which most resemble other works with which one is already familiar. But when those parts have receded, we can still be captivated by another phrase which, because its shape had been too novel to let our mind see anything there but confusion, had been made undetectable and kept intact; and the phrase we passed by every day unawares, the phrase which had withheld itself, which by the sheer power of its own beauty had become invisible and remained unknown to us, is the one which comes to us last of all. But it will also be the last one we leave. We shall love it longer than the others, because we took longer to love it.

As I said, Proust here gives art priority over human beauty, of which our experience proceeds in exactly the opposite direction. But then, he didn't listen to Jutta.

For what Jutta describes is undoubtedly a fulfilment, a long-lasting, subjectively almost endless and thus truly paradisiacal bliss, something entirely euphoric—that's how Jutta portrays it—whose intensity and physical immersion apparently surpass any experience I've had in bed or in the concert hall. She herself says that the feeling is most similar to the intoxicating joy that took hold of her after the birth of her children, except that this was mixed with such exhaustion that she can't entirely call it joy, and it was maybe more like relief; she still felt such fear for her baby, as well as the pain, which reliably made her scream in each delivery room that she couldn't go on, and swear that this was definitely the last time. Even afterwards, she only gradually got used to the idea of getting pregnant again; she really had to force herself and suppress her memory of the ordeal, whereas the bliss that tantra allows her to experience already calls out for the next time before it's over, a sense of again-and-again and even-more-and-more.

No, I mustn't imagine it like normal sex, Jutta emphasizes; the difference is quite simply that you don't have an orgasm in the usual sense, a kind of climax or, for men, an actual ejaculation; through specific, absolutely learnable breathing techniques that develop more and more with repetition, a deep, abrupt inhalation and exhalation at the exact moment when you think you can't control your arousal any more, the orgasm is simultaneously stopped and preserved, but far more than just preserved: an immense, almighty wave of pleasantly cool air seems to break over you and enter you from above—not through the mouth or the nose but from the top of the skull, first into the head, with such force that you literally don't know what's happening to you at first, it's like being hit by a wave and tossed around—but in a good way, without any fear! From the head, the air flows so quickly that you can feel it at every point, through your whole body to the fingers and the feet, so that your limbs twitch about as if you were having an epileptic fit—as a teacher, she had observed it often enough from the outside—and you cry out as piercingly as a woman in labour, but out of joy, not pain, even if the two are indistinguishable to the observer.

'So a church congress really might not be the most suitable place to practise tantra,' Jutta adds.

'It's still more bearable than the songs there,' I say in an attempt at humour.

Then Jutta becomes serious: when it happens—and even she doesn't get there every time, which is why she always feels that it's a miracle when it does happen, and is amazed that such joy even exists in life—when it happens, it leaves her with such tenderness, such a universal love, not focused on an individual person but encompassing the whole world, that, as soon as she has control of her limbs again, she wants to hold onto the one person who happens to be next to her, and actually hugs them or even kisses their hands in gratitude, if she knows them reasonably well.

I'm not sure what to make of Jutta's divine sex, whatever unimagined sensations it promises. But—the thought comes to me when Jutta pauses for a moment—the fact that a tantrist can become a mayor these days is pretty terrific. When we were growing up there were no women to be seen anywhere in politics—okay, maybe a minister for family affairs or health here and there, but no one in a leading position, least of all in our provincial area. Only 30 years have passed since then, and if Jutta were lesbian, had a different religion, were disabled, non-white, intersex or into BDSM, it would probably be tolerated too. And another thing: the state she fought against in Brokdorf—now she *is* that state. It could be that she's no more noble-minded or useful to the public than the mayors, head teachers or federal chancellors who were automatically her opponents, at best negotiating partners, well-meaning or intolerable representatives of an alien, essentially hostile system that needed to be dismantled. With today's eyes, she would show more understanding, perhaps even a degree of acknowledgement to those same mayors, head teachers or chancellors she once attacked as reactionaries. Yes, I'm sure she herself has changed more than the country has, that she now accepts it as her own, and maybe even more than that, even if she wouldn't use the same words: that she loves it, loves Germany.

Just these two words together still sound unseemly today, and love is the last thing that someone like Jutta would have associated with Germany 30 years ago. A country can't change as quickly as a person changes in 30 years; it doesn't leave home for good and become a mother, doesn't arrange a flat for the first time, doesn't weep from lovesickness or cry out with joy, doesn't worry about the children or stand at its parents' grave, doesn't gradually grow older than it ever remembers its parents being. What I mean is that I'm impressed by the élan with which Jutta talks about her work, I fundamentally appreciate her efforts to improve her own immediate surroundings—but I hope I'm not overly romanticizing that second grass pitch and the healthy fair trade breakfast at school. She wouldn't deny her own ambition to be re-elected, because power, including the official car, is more stimulating than six patients an hour. It's more the satisfaction that one of us is sitting in that car, while those who have something against lesbians, people of different faiths, the disabled, people of colour, intersex people or BDSM fans have to reject the order that is now in place; better for them to feel marginalized, to see conspiracy theories around every corner and view the public sphere as manipulated than for us to still be in that position.

'I haven't read such a pile of apologist shit in a long time,' the editor will groan, who sees Jutta without my loving eye.

'Apologist?' I will ask.

'Yes, apologist,' the editor will affirm, and email me a link to an essay describing the class struggle of a middle and upper class with an authoritarian ecological bent. Everything one is supposed to condemn in society today is attributed to the sub-proletariat: they smoke and drink too much, they've got too much meat on their plates, they're too fat and don't exercise enough, they worship cars, don't cycle enough and, on top of that, work for industries the country would be better off without. Plus they have lots of children, and they're stupid as well. And they go on holiday in the wrong places, where they turn up in excessive numbers and behave badly to boot. This neo-Protestantism brooks no dissent; its sharpest weapons are the brutal denigration of all other ways of life and an unprecedented cultural colonialism.

Tantra prolonged her marriage, Jutta says into the silence that I didn't end in time, before lapsing into gloominess: tantra and children, those are the only shared projects in her marriage. Evidently her thoughts have returned to her living room and

she's discovered the crisp bags again, lying open on the coffee
table and scattered on the floor, the half-full cereal bowl and the
DVDs of American films her husband always gets worked up
about; she has also seen me, discovered me, practically a stranger,
whom she's told more about herself within a few hours than she's
told her husband in the last ten years; she has thought of her husband, who will have gone to bed by now, without even saying
good night—but if he had actually entered the living room, she
would have rebuffed any attempt at reconciliation so soon after
their quarrel, which wasn't even one, if only out of bafflement.
Not openly, of course, not in front of this stranger; a noticeable
coolness in her reciprocation of his greeting would have been
sufficient to grant her a brief triumph. Then his shoulders would
have hinted at a resigned shrug, and he would have gone to sleep
with the good feeling that it really wasn't because of him, while
she would have compounded her ire by being angry at herself.
It would have taken days, if not weeks, for her to be worn down
to the point where she'd smile at him on meeting him in the
kitchen or while brushing her teeth, or where she'd put her hand
on his forearm, only to take revenge at the most inopportune
moment for the greater triumph she had thus allowed him. In
love, the same as between peoples, it's always the other person's
fault, otherwise we couldn't feel so comfortable with our hurt
egos: if the other person were just a little more understanding, a
little more caring, more sensitive or more moderate in their
expectations, if they had paid attention back then, when the
sorrow, stress or whatever was visible in your face—my God,
it's already been 15 years—if you hadn't been brusquely dis-
missed when you took a step towards them before—five minutes

later, sadly, it was too late. 'What we call experience is only the revelation to our own eyes of one of our own character traits,' Proust remarks concerning the mistakes in love from which one never learns. 'The kind of plagiarism which it is most difficult for any human individual to avoid (and even for whole nations, who persist in reproducing their faults and aggravate them in so doing) is self-plagiarism.'

Certainly the alcohol is also contributing; she emptied the second bottle almost by herself too, after which she yet again started listing, almost like a bookkeeper—I'm sick of hearing it—how much she and her husband used to have in common and all the things that separate them now, starting with her political pragmatism, which he positively despises, and the general practice, which she found unconvincing, but she couldn't think of an alternative with two small children; then his obsession with sport, her Christian faith and even the Alps, as if the Alps were to blame for their marital problems, she'd rather go to the city more often, to the opera, to the theatre. She'd also like to eat meat at home again, not just at work-related events. And her political office in general, which he can't take seriously.

'We always wanted to be equals,' Jutta complains. 'On an equal footing, that was the idea.'

As I said, I find this enumeration rather tiring; but not just tiring, suddenly I also dislike the facial expression she assumes, the way the presses her lips together between two sentences or half-sentences, the way the corners of her move have dropped. If someone took a snapshot now, she wouldn't even look attractive to a loving eye any more, just morose, gloomy and old beyond her years. Strange that both the greatest pleasure and annoyance, let alone anger and hate—which I am not ascribing to Jutta, I just mean the principle—can so disfigure a face, any face, whereas we seem most beautiful when we are indifferent, or at most compassionate, like the mother of God. After all, compassion or sympathy, which we wear so well in paintings and snapshots, are no more than secondary emotions; someone else is feeling, someone else is suffering, and one only feels and suffers with them. Doesn't that say something unsettling about our longing, namely that we find those people more attractive who are not fulfilled themselves?

The editor will not only scrap the list of commonalities that have disappeared from the marriage over the years, and will only allow a cursory mention of the separating elements; more than that, he will also predict almost verbatim the objections that Jutta will make to his cuts. He's a good and experienced editor, the best I know; I'd hardly put up with his abuse if he weren't. He knows my narcissistic insistence on every single word. To butter me up, he'll start by claiming that he thought about a statement of mine . . .

'Which statement?' I'll ask.

. . . somewhere earlier in the novel, of which I'll already have written the first draft by then, this statement: that the first sentence of *Anna Karenina* isn't true.

'That all happy marriages are similar, while each unhappy marriage is unhappy in its own particular way?'

Aside from the fact, the editor will say, that, if we're being consistent, a Russian writer like Tolstoy doesn't belong in a novel that takes French literature as its frame of reference . . .

'Well . . . ' I will sigh, drawing out the word until even the editor stops being so serious about consistency.

. . . and Tolstoy doesn't speak of 'marriages' either, but of 'families' . . .

'Oh right,' I will stammer and feel ashamed, as I do so often in front of my reader, who will pick up any little attempt to cheat.

. . . so, leaving aside my poetological and philological sloppiness, which he will never get used to, I would actually be right: the few happy marriages he knows all have some secret, because their happiness seems inexplicable from the outside. By contrast, the unhappy ones are unhappy—not for the same reasons, he wouldn't go that far, but for obvious reasons that differ more in their social circumstances than particularities of character. Jutta's marital crisis is the most ordinary kind of all, often found in novels set in today's prosperous societies—in fact, it's practically stereotypical for that milieu and age, he wants me to explain to Jutta, and tell her frankly that that was exactly why I chose her as the subject of my novel: because her case is generalizable.

'I don't find Jutta all that ordinary,' I will say in her defence and in defence of my longing, and also, perhaps unconsciously, the novel I am writing: 'A German female mayor who also teaches the Indian art of love.'

The editor will remain unimpressed: 'It could just as easily be triathlon or Tai Chi; the uniform of individualism is its non-conformity.'

Whatever items she has on her list are interchangeable, he wants me to tell Jutta when she insists on some unusual circumstances—'Interchangeable!' the editor will exclaim so vehemently that I will wonder how his own marriage is faring. For Jutta it's the exercise she's too lazy to keep up, for someone else it's the city trips he can't be bothered to go on. Or the reading! Or the food! Or the sex! Or the parenting! Or the TV programme! Or the beer belly! Or the migraines! What is this anyway, the editor will ask, what does Jutta expect? She met her husband through some coincidences or other in her mid-twenties and fell in love with him, fine, but should the two of them just have stopped moving so that their precious commonalities would remain untouched, could one walk through life holding hands? Of course two lovers will keep developing and will move in different directions; the question is only whether they will stay within sight of each other.

'Within sight?' I will ask.

'Yes, within sight,' the editor will affirm, and try to convince me to get rid of the worn-out phrase 'on an equal footing' . . .

'But I don't say that, Jutta says it.'

. . . which, no matter who says it, is a no-go in a novel.

'Well,' I will play it down again, 'weeell . . . ' and with the reference to a 'no-go'—the novelist can go anywhere, anywhere at all, and that includes petty acts of spite—I will put a word in his mouth that will annoy him far more.

And what's this whole idea anyway, the editor will fume more and more, equal footing, equal footing—if one always wants to stay on an equal footing then one can never stoop or shrink or grow or jump or kneel or rest and lie down or just turn over, one has to stay rooted to the spot. And that's terror, terror through equality, because it's very rare for two partners to be the same size, it's already rare physically but even rarer inwardly, and it changes over the years too, then one of them has to stretch idiotically or the other one has to adopt a silly stoop, one of them has to be cramped or the other one bent. Or vice versa, but almost never equal! By now the editor will be ranting unstoppably, and, because I now make a point of asking him, will actually speak from his own personal experience—not about his own marriage, though, but that of his late parents, whose sex life was certainly nothing sensational. Even as a young married couple, they never had much in common, barely knew each other when they got married, the way it was back then—they went to a cafe a few times to eat cake together, went dancing twice, there was secret hand holding and excited kisses; something we'd consider no more than a flirt today was enough to pass as a marriage of love. And their marriage didn't even feature two projects, it was just the children from the start. Aside from that, he had a job at the firm and she did the housework. After supper, he'd go to the village pub and she would snuggle up in front of the television; he'd come home after the last round, while she was already asleep by ten.

Once the children were out of the house, she wanted a divorce and so did he, really, but they stayed married, maybe just for tax reasons or because they didn't know what to do with the house. He made a rather makeshift accommodation out of the first floor, where the bedrooms had been, while she turned the ground floor into a modern, and actually very tasteful flat; to the children, it seemed like she only really started living then. They put separate nameplates on their respective front doors, and whenever the editor came home, he first rang the bell on the ground floor to visit his mother, only going upstairs after that. It was only on festive days, when all the children came, that his mother cooked for the whole family and his father appeared at the door like a friendly neighbour with a bunch of flowers, and at Christmas with a handsomely wrapped gift.

After a few years, his parents started eating together again—regularly, not every day, but whenever one of the children came to visit. Aside from that, they continued to live seemingly separate lives—but they weren't separate, the editor will emphasize, not completely separate. They stayed within sight of each other. When they needed each other, or rather when the father needed the mother—but he would have taken care of her just as naturally, and yes, lovingly, because it was love, the editor will exclaim with moist eyes—when they needed each other, they were there for each other. First she cooked for him every day and went shopping for him, then their doors stayed open the whole time, and at the end, which still lasted another five or six years—and for all the pain and trials they were good years, the editor will insist, maybe even the best—at the end his mother took in his father, who couldn't climb stairs any more, and they lived together, still in separate rooms, but with a far more intimate bond than they ever had when they shared a bed. The father, who no longer had any expenses because he barely left the house, rented out the first floor and had the money paid into her account so that she would at least have some financial benefit if she was already looking after him. She should be able to enjoy life a little, the father always said. The mother, whom everyone assumed to be in good health, died soon after him.

I don't want to know about any of that. I don't want to know when he last went along to her parents and how often she went along to his, who admittedly live nearby; that was the only reason he had bought the surgery so cheaply. I don't want to hear about how arrogantly he grabbed the hardest cases for himself when they used to work together, and she would often feel like an idiot, like a nurse, in front of the patients, let alone the staff. I don't want to know that of all those emancipatory dogmas, the only one he gave up was sitting down to pee. I don't want to know that it took him over an hour to be with her when they got the news of her father's death because he didn't want to send home the patients who were already in the waiting room, and he didn't cancel his afternoon appointments either. I don't want to know whether he got home just a few minutes earlier than usual or a whole hour, as he's claimed ever since, don't want to know if he mentioned in a normal tone of voice that he wasn't going to tennis today, or announced it so ostentatiously that Jutta, who'd been in tears the whole time, could only scream at him to fuck off out of her life and didn't even care if the children heard them arguing. I don't want to know how cruelly he rubs it in when he's obviously in the right, when she yells at him in front of the kids, sometimes for rather trivial reasons, or completely forgets the parents' evening or commits God knows what unspeakable crime; after all, he's godlike in his perfection. And it's not as if he confronts her about it; no, no, if he knows very well that she knows she messed up, he wisely refrains from reproaching her because he knows—always bloody knows it all, he was already a smart-arse in the jungle, she sees it with hindsight—because he knows very well that she knows he knows she knows, and reproaches herself much more harshly than if he reproached her, because that would immediately get her defences up and she'd reproach him back, which might be justified because he's not really as godlike as all that, but if he doesn't reproach her then she can't defend herself, then she's defenceless and his unspoken reproaches will rain down on her as self-reproaches, and then she cries in bed at night in the unacknowledged hope that he'll take her in his arms, but he doesn't take her in his arms, he never takes her in his arms when she cries in bed, no, he goes one better when, because she needs some counter-reproaches again, she complains weeks later that he turned around and was snoring again after three minutes—his snoring is another thing—while she cried in bed, then he goes one better and accuses her of emotional blackmail, which he won't submit to, he can't take her in his arms if he's justifiably angry with her, or unjustifiably too, okay, he has his emotions too after all, it's not always just her, and his feelings can get hurt too, believe it or not. And however indignantly she rejects the accusation of blackmail, she knows that he's not entirely wrong, and he knows that she knows it, so he can turn over again and snore contentedly. Doesn't she snore? I don't want to know, nor do I want to know that he always rearranges the dishes after she puts them in the dishwasher to fit more in, don't want to know that he gets the bathroom sink filthy every night with the maté tea he drinks at his desk, instead of emptying the pot into the toilet or, even better, taking it to the kitchen. I don't want to know that he doesn't accompany to official occasions on principle, and wasn't even there for her inauguration, the children were but he wasn't, even though people have started gossiping and as much as she sometimes wants him there, needs him there at this or that dinner, just to know that he's there or that she has someone she can talk to, whisper to or smile at mischievously when she's surrounded by ghastly people, only last week the Lions Club, lots of well-fed, self-satisfied, openly sexist men with her as the only woman, the horror, the naked horror, but she has to grin and bear it to keep the publisher of the local newspaper on side—he praised her in front of everyone as a good girl, just imagine it: she, the mayor, was a good girl; he'd never have dared to do that if her husband had been sitting next to her, but her husband never sits next to her, he refuses to sit next to her, because he'd sooner blow up the Lions Club than go to the Lions Club or the rifle club or the championship party at the football club, where they gave her one beer shower after another; he refuses, not because he has contempt for her work, but because it just doesn't interest him, because he doesn't think separate rubbish bins will save the world and even considers sensor-controlled traffic lights decidedly wrong, the wrong message to send, people should switch to cycling or use public transport, but try telling a commuter here that they should switch to cycling, tell them that a petrol price of five or eight euros would be realistic to cover the cost for the environment and the community, but then he says it's precisely our dependence on oil that constantly forces into new wars and our alliance with Saudi Arabia, although Saudi Arabia spreads jihadist ideology, which the West doesn't fight but deliberately inflames with its Middle East policy, because after the end of the Soviet Union . . .

'What about you, where do you think the terror come from?' Jutta suddenly asks.

'Excuse me?'

'The terror, where does it come from?'

When the culture office books someone like me for a literary event, they don't just get integration as part of the package. Conveniently enough, my background also makes me an expert on terror. They don't mean any harm, of course; they're sincerely interested, just as they want to know from Albert Bloch, however little he might differ from other people, what it's like being an Israelite. And there's never a salon where he isn't asked about the Dreyfus Affair. And with someone like Bloch one could tell by his complexion, however hard he tried. Even the novelist has to emphasize that Bloch is a Frenchman. 'Ah!' Monsieur de Charlus innocently apologizes, 'I thought he was a Jew.' People ask him in the most cordial tone whether he wants to go back to his home country. That isn't necessarily an expression of racism; their curiosity comes simply from 'aesthetic interest and love of local colour', as Proust writes in *Lost Time*.

> The Romanians, the Egyptians, the Turks may hate the Jews. But in a French salon the differences between those peoples are not so evident, and a Jew making his entry as though he were coming in from some remote part of the desert, his body bent forward like a hyena, his neck sloped forward, offering effusive 'salaams', satisfies in every way a taste for things oriental.

'But you, with your mystics, you go "salaam salaam" all the time too,' Jutta will remind me with reference to the novel I read from tonight.

'That's true,' I will concede, 'but what was I supposed to do if I just wanted to write about mysticism—should I have gone for Hildegard of Bingen, just to defy expectations?'

'But now you're going for Proust after all?'

'No, not because of that,' I will insist. 'I love Proust. Someone like me just has to love Proust.

I read somewhere that Proust felt the most affection towards him, the Jew Albert Bloch, and I was surprised. After all, Proust writes: 'Finer friendships than Bloch's—which is not saying much', he concludes in *Lost Time*. 'He had all the failings that I disliked.' Bloch is characterized as lachrymose, vulgar and boastful, as an oaf whose overzealousness leads him to commit one social faux pas after another. He elbows his way to the front at every salon, adopts the current majority opinion, wants to belong at all costs and will even speak like an anti-Semite himself to curry favour with others. Yes, he loves classical music and poetry, but shows off his education because he wants to do things so well, speaks so stiltedly that people laugh at him, and gets worked up too quickly; he probably gesticulates wildly while speaking too, like all Mediterranean types.

And yet what I read was true, as I gradually realized: the novelist treats Swann more as a role model and object of admiration, while his friendship with Saint-Loup peters out such that his death is mentioned almost in passing. Only Bloch remains until the end. 'For me, who had known him on the threshold of

his life and always pictured him thus, he was my school-friend,'
says the aged novelist, although it is clear from the descriptions
of those childhood days what makes him so tiring. 'Bloch was
not invited to the house again'—this was not because of his
Jewishness but his eccentric behaviour.

> At first he had been made quite welcome. It was true that
> my grandfather claimed that each time I formed a closer
> attachment to one of my friends than the others and
> brought him home, he was always a Jew, which would
> not have displeased him—even his friend Swann was of
> Jewish extraction—had he not felt that it was not from
> among the best that I had chosen him. And so when I
> brought home a new friend, he very seldom failed to
> hum: 'Oh God of our Fathers' from *La Juive* or 'Israel,
> break they bond', singing only the tune, naturally (Ti la
> lam talam, talim), but I was afraid my friend would know
> it and restore the words.
>
> Before he saw them, simply from hearing the name,
> which quite often had nothing particularly Jewish about
> it, he would guess not only the Jewish background of
> those of my friends who were in fact Jewish, but even
> whatever might be distressing about their family.
>
> 'And what is the name of this friend of yours who's
> coming this evening?'
>
> 'Dumont, Grandfather.'
>
> 'Dumont! Oh, now I'm suspicious!'
>
> And he would sing:
>
> Archers, be on your guard!
> Watch without rest, without sound.

And after adroitly asking us a few more specific questions, he would cry out: 'On guard! On guard!' or, if it was the victim himself, already there, whom he had forced, by a subtle interrogation, unwittingly to confess his origins, then, to show us he no longer had any doubts, he would simply gaze at us while barely perceptibly humming:

Let you now guide
The steps of this timid Israelite!

When Jutta reads the novel, she will accuse me of turning the Muslim into the new Jew. At first I won't understand what she means, since I don't make any comparisons, don't say anything about criticisms of Islam, and specifically avoid discussing something like the new Houellebecq that she's foisting on me. But then I'll concede that any consideration of the anti-Semitism described in Lost Time practically insinuates the comparison.

'Don't you start talking as pompously as Bloch,' the editor will say in a similar vein.

'Can't you all leave me in peace!' I will exclaim, driving the editor out of that paragraph, of which I'll only accept Jutta's criticism.

Because yes, it's simply true that many of the things said about Jews in Lost Time are identical to things one can pick up today, even in the salons and festivities of the literary scene, for example: 'You know I don't have any personal racial prejudices, I don't think that fits into our times,' undoubtedly followed by a real whopper; the handshake I have been openly refused too, as if it would make someone dirty; the taboo-breaking gesture with which one voices the most common opinions; the Jewish chief witness that anti-Semitism needs for its accusations in order to hide its racism; the libidinousness and thus animality of the oriental; the question of whether Judaism is part of France, as if there were no Jewish Frenchmen and women; and finally the fear of a 'Jewish invasion', which statistics and biblical exegesis show already led to the decline of the West in the early 20th century: 'I'm not opposed to Judaism per se, but there are just too many here.' And always the question of one's background, always the country before the hyphen, something-German, as much as I'd like to delete the nationality from announcements or Wikipedia, because no one cares when people are simply German; always the reference to religion, even when it's totally inappropriate, to the point where the reader would even think that if I learnt tantrism, it would be an expression or a rejection of my faith: 'When we meet orientals in society, whether they belong to one group or another, it feels as if we were facing supernatural creatures that manifest themselves through the power of spiritism.'

As I said, that's by no means necessarily an expression of ressentiment, in Germany today, in educated circles, and maybe it actually isn't in the majority of cases; as with Dreyfus's supporters, this fetishism of origins is practised today as much, or even more, by those who open themselves up to foreign things, whether it's belly dance or refugee relief. 'Perhaps you could ask your friend to get me invited to some attractive festival in the Temple, a circumcision, or some Jewish chants,' says Monsieur de Charlus, who does not consider Dreyfus guilty of treason because a Jew cannot have France as his homeland, to express his sincere interest in foreign culture.

You might even arrange some comic turns. For instance,
a contest between your friend and his father, in which he
would smite him as David smote Goliath. That would
make quite an amusing farce.

'What, have you totally lost the plot now?' Jutta will ask when
she reads the novel, pointing to the Paris attacks, the persecution
of Christians in the Middle East and the obstacles to integration
she comes up against on a daily basis in her work as mayor, the
women who have lived in Germany for 40 years but still walk a
metre behind the men, the schoolboys who don't respect any
female teachers. 'Believe me, I meet a lot of Muslims, and they're
often incredibly nice people. But isn't Islam, pardon my French,
a bit of a fucked-up religion?'

'Oof,' I will sigh, and not even bother trying to come up with
a response; I can't think of one spontaneously anyway.

'And you get pampered and spoilt here,' Jutta will rage
uncontrollably, 'you have every kind of right, the right to vote,
health insurance, unemployment benefit, you get invited
specifically because you're a Muslim, and in our little shithole
you'd be very welcome to give a New Year's address. You can't
seriously compare that to the situation of Jews. I mean, I'm the
one around here who's pushing for the mosque. Do you have
any idea what you're saying?'

'But I'm not even saying that.'

'So why did you write it in your novel?'

Even without knowing about Jutta's reservations, which she will
quickly soften, as she has a knack for nuances, I really don't want

to talk about terror now; I hear our dissonance in the very word, and prefer to think of the receptive mode I was in for most of the evening. I just need to finally find the button.

'Only a moment ago you were speaking beautifully about making love,' I say, bringing the conversation back to the topic that interests someone like me most—that's apparently what Houellebecq says about the libidinous oriental, if what I heard about the novel that Jutta would have brought up again next is true.

'Yes, so?' Jutta asks, not realizing what I'm getting at.

'How many marriages have something like that?' I ask, referring to the sexual stability that still exists in their marriage after 20 years.

'But we worked on it too,' Jutta says, with the same diction she found so awful before.

She wasn't the one who started tantra; it was him, when they were only making love in the dark, under the covers and quietly, becoming more and more workmanlike and ultimately so unimaginative that one could hardly use the word any more. They were tired enough from being on call, doing what were effectively 48-hour shifts, and when one of them finally came home, the other was just going to work and vice versa. Someone had to be there with the kids, after all; kindergarten was only for ages three and up, and was only open till 12. There was feminism, but no all-day childcare yet. But he was just as involved in the parenting duties as she was, maybe even more, and did every-thing to ensure that she didn't neglect her work, though he seemed to take it less and less seriously—so she claims, but he would deny it. More than that, he would be outraged by the accusation and accuse her of being *so* unfair, when he had always stood behind her so that she could go her own way. Maybe, she would think, but perhaps it was just part of his emancipatory self-image to have a working wife, or he just wanted to keep her busy, because for men it feels like a gift that they can finally be fathers—as long as the cleaner takes care of the toilet, assuming there's no wife, mistress or female comrade; it's not only separate rubbish bins and healthy eating that need a middle-class income, but equal opportunities too.

'It was hard at first,' Jutta recalls, thinking of her first tantric workshop: all the participants naked on yoga cushions in a circle, and then they had to form pairs—not with their own partners, and same-sex pairs were all the better. But because the men who didn't get a woman were embarrassed, Jutta was separated from the woman she had, whom it seemed less sinful to massage. Sinful? Squatter or not, at the end of the day she came from a pietistic village, and was following this alternative life model more out of Christian conviction than dialectical insight.

Jutta mumbled short prayers as she lay stretched out in front of a stranger, who was supposed to arouse her in imaginative ways at the female teacher's instruction, and thought of her husband, who she was sure had no problems about cuddling with a strange woman, and everyone watched—and listened to!—them. It was only when she had to kneel with a feather in her hand next to the stranger, who was bearded to boot and as fat as a bear, with body hair like fur—it was no coincidence that he was the last man left—that she gave a sob, not just out of shame, but even more out of anger. To top it all, the bear was one of those do-gooders who prefer a natural smell to deodorant.

'What on earth am I doing here?' Jutta had asked herself; the question still seemed appropriate 20 years later, as I had to think of my editor, who is also fat and bearded.

The instructor knelt down beside and embraced her as if they were best friends, asking her if something was wrong; but how was she supposed to explain in front of everyone that she was repelled by this bearded man, who was waiting with closed eyes to be aroused imaginatively? Or even whisper in the instructor's ear that she found moaning in a circle perverted, all those aroused cocks and spread women's legs? How to explain to her why she was angry at her husband? 'Don't be such a square', he'd pestered her when they read the brochure together, and waxed lyrical about Indian religiosity, which wasn't as prudish as her Protestantism. No: she couldn't admit, not back then, that she was jealous, because jealousy was the squarest thing of all in her generation, she couldn't explain the nightmare to anyone, when part of the nightmare is that one can't wake up and turn on the light.

But she did learn sex as a sacrament in the end, later on, differently and without her husband, who knew her well enough to see what she thought of the workshop even with his eyes closed. What had relieved her almost more than his understanding was finding out that he felt just as uncomfortable. After a glance at each other and two whispered sentences, they agreed to pick up their yoga cushions and pick up the children early from the grandparents. On the drive there he kept apologizing for the torment he'd forced her to endure, and assured her that the Indian art of love would be his first and last attempt to be especially imaginative. They could just as easily free up some space themselves, treat themselves to a weekend trip or take the morning off so that they'd be undisturbed and well-rested in bed. At the motorway rest area they burst out laughing so hard that they almost spat out the schnitzel they indulged in after that spirituality (back then he still ate meat). They couldn't eat for minutes, bent over with laughter on the benches opposite, and when they sat up again they snorted snatches of words across the table, or at best half-sentences, that didn't need to be intelligible to conjure up further details of the fiasco. Even the truck drivers at the next table joined in the laughter at some point, so they must have made a funny sight, these two young lovebirds—or so they thought—and the four of them had a smoke and a few shots, which they remembered being available at rest areas back then along with ashtrays.

Later, without asking her, he turned off the motorway. She assumed he was tired or wanted to avoid a breath test. Actually, he was looking for a hotel to make use of the free space created by the abandoned workshop. The children weren't expecting them until Sunday.

There's one question I can't get out of my head: why did Jutta, who rails against sexual repression and doesn't just sanctify physical pleasure but even preaches it, and until recently even preached it in public—why didn't she say a word in response to the confession of the schoolmate she met at the church congress, even though she had dreamt of him for weeks?

'Because I'm faithful,' Jutta replies.

'Huh?' I exclaim—not quite as affectedly as Albert Bloch, but I simply can't make sense of a monogamy that accommodates sex in a circle of chairs.

With the face of a teacher whose pupil has given the wrong answer yet again, Jutta points out that at a workshop, firstly, no one sits in chairs, and secondly, there's no intercourse, the team leaders make sure of that. Even the word 'lovemaking', which she normally uses so excessively, is misleading in the context of tantra because it's not about love in the usual sense.

'So you just have sex?' I try to understand her with my no doubt very uptight mind.

'No one has sex,' Jutta corrects me.

'Eh?'

It's not so easy for me to understand why, from Jutta's surely very open point of view, an orgiastic business like tantra doesn't violate the principle of fidelity, which she takes equally seriously. It's about oneself, she explains, about the God in you. Well, what am I supposed to say to that? The tantrist simply offers help, Jutta continues, as she can see the next question in my face. She—most professional tantrists are women—is more like a servant, she doesn't share the experience herself.

'So it's more of a service?' I enquire, because I don't dare to ask if it doesn't essentially amount to prostitution if there's payment involved.

'I see it more as something therapeutic.'

Of course, it helps if there's a certain sympathy between the tantrist and her customer . . .

'Customer?'

'It's a market too, sure.'

. . . but she doesn't have to love them, any more than a psychologist loves a patient or a priest their congregation.

'What kind of market?'

'You wouldn't believe how many shady outfits there are.'

The tantrist doesn't even have to be good-looking; good looks can even be an impediment, as they distract customers from themselves. And she has no problem with giving a massage to someone who's ugly or even crippled. On the contrary: it's especially rewarding when she helps someone who's never slept with a woman to live out his sexuality, like a disabled person who may not be able to in the normal sense. Then it's something special for her too and she really enjoys it. And it's arousing too, in a very particular way.

'And you've never slept with another man?'

'Not since I've been married.'

I'm not sure whether to believe her. At the end of high school she certainly had no reservations about taking a 15-year-old to her room in the shared flat, and 'fidelity' was generally as much of a taboo word as 'jealousy' in her generation, our generation. On the other hand, she had a strict pietistic upbringing, and that's putting it harmlessly; they were sects, these villages all around our city, real sects, cut off from the world, all the women and even the girls wearing the same grey felt skirts and frilly blouses, all the men in pleated trousers and shirts buttoned up to the top. She found it so awful, I remind Jutta, that she fled to the squat before she'd even finished school.

'I found some things awful, not all of it. At some point you realize that there were a few good things too: the equality, the contentment, the respect for life. And the songs are really lovely too. You realize that it's just part of who you are. And that you don't necessarily have to reject that part. That you can take your own path without tearing down everything behind you.

What Jutta finds more awful than pietism today is promiscuity, when everyone does it with everyone else and sexuality loses its preciousness; she sees what goes on, sees it in her shitty backwater too. Without her training, she too might have ended up in some hotel bed with the local bank manager.

'In all religions, sexuality is something sacred,' Jutta announces with a sudden solemnity that, in the nocturnal living room, between cereal bowls and a football jersey, sounds even stranger than her politician's tone. 'It's precisely because it's sacred that it has to be protected and restricted.'

'But you dreamt of the bishop at night.'

If I understood her correctly, Jutta declared desire to be practically the highest feeling of all, stimulated with such sophistication that even the hair becomes an erogenous zone, whereas the act that the rest of us view as fulfilment isn't considered especially important or even aimed for.

'You could've just told the bishop how you felt. It needn't have led to anything.'

'But I didn't want to feel like that.'

Now she starts going on about Saint Paul again, who's still in the way when she tries to combine Christianity with tantra and tantra with fidelity, but not just fidelity, also self-denial—what a circle! The arguments and biblical passages she uses seem so arbitrarily chosen, their combination so abstruse, that I actually start explaining Christianity to her. But with our speech probably slurred from intoxication or sleepiness, we don't manage to formulate a single statement that will stand up to scrutiny in the morning. My editor, however, will send me *Diary of a Country Priest* by Georges Bernanos, which has been out of print in Germany for decades. 'Purity', Bernanos writes—and Jutta would probably apply this to fidelity, as love is a religious matter for her—

> ... purity is not prescribed to us, like a punishment, it is one of the mysterious but obvious conditions—as experience confirms—of that metaphysical knowledge of oneself, knowledge of oneself in God, that we call faith. Impurity does not destroy this knowledge, it wipes out the need for it. People have stopped believing because they have lost the desire to believe. You have lost the desire to know yourselves. This profound truth, your truth, no longer interests you. You may say that the dogmas you used to accept are still present in your thoughts, and that only reason rejects them. No matter! We only really possess what we desire [ ... ].

I will really get stuck into Bernanos, whose religious pathos can only be understood in opposition to the radical secularism of the French society novel, as the editor writes in his accompanying letter; German literature, infused with metaphysical references that move away from Christianity, and authored conspicuously often by sons of priests, would at most have produced a *Diary of a Country Priest* as a grotesque. Bernanos, however, approaches Christianity very strictly. To be honest, I won't be entirely sure if his novel fits into mine, which is perhaps not so much the reason for my readings as the form they take; the amount of experience that flows into literature in proportion to what one has read about is vastly overestimated anyway, so I'll just keep quoting merrily . . .

'You can't do that!' the editor will write in red in the margin, as the novel already has too many digressions.

. . . because *Diary of a Country Priest* explains what is pleasurable about Christianity so much more convincingly than Jutta.

'You were the one who sent me the Bernanos,' I will note in the revised version to fob off the editor.

'The opposite of a Christian nation is a sad nation,' says the novelist's spiritual mentor, the old vicar of Torcy, formulating an idea that is similar to Jutta's and already baffled people 80 years ago: 'You may say the definition isn't particularly theological. True.' And, just like Jutta, the vicar of Torcy refers to the gloominess of typical church services, which only made people yawn, and the catechism, which drives the enjoyment out of religion once and for all. And yet the church need only remember early childhood, which we experienced as so sweet and radiant even though we were defenceless against pain, sadness and illness and completely dependent:

> But it is from his own sense of helplessness that the child humbly derives the very principle of his joy. He relates it to his mother, don't you see?

Outside of the church, a nation would always remain a dis-
possessed nation, a nation of foundlings. In the church, however,
each person learns—could learn, if the masses weren't so boring
and the catechism so dry!—that they are a child of God. They
could live with this knowledge in their head and die with this
reassurance—and that would not be something learnt, for it
would be a basic trust pervading and animating the daily tasks,
distractions and entertainments, even the most ordinary needs.
The farmer would continue to plough the earth, the scholar
would hunch over his tablets, the engineer would produce his
devices, and each would still bear their share of trouble, hunger
and thirst, misery and jealousy—but a different church from the
existing one would stop people feeling lost. Whoever doesn't
believe in the living God can put their boots in front of the fire-
place in the hope of fulfilment; the devil is tired of putting a load
of mechanical toys in them as presents, playthings that go out of
fashion as soon as they are invented, in the end just tiny packets
of cocaine, heroin or morphine that don't cost him much.

> Poor fellows! They will have wearied even sin. Not
> everyone is good at amusing himself. The cheapest of
> cheap dolls keeps a child happy for a whole season, while
> an old man will yawn over a toy that costs five hundred
> francs. Why? Because he's lost his childlike spirit. Well,
> the Church has been given the task by the Lord of
> maintaining that childlike spirit in the world, that
> innocence, that freshness.

The editor is right: the books are starting to take over. But what
can I do if literature ultimately interests me more than what really

happens? And with Bernanos there's the additional factor that I didn't know him before and want to finish reading him first.

'Finish reading it,' the editor will scold me, 'take a break from Jutta as long as you like, but don't go on about everything that's important to you.'

Yes, I will think while the editor continues his customary lecture, that's exactly what the novel I am writing is meant to be, all novels, the whole of life: what's important to me now.

Well then: paganism is no enemy of nature, Bernanos concedes, but only Christianity lends greatness to nature and relates it correctly to humans, to what humans dream of. Only the church—a different church, one that Jutta preaches in a different setting, but with similar words—only the church can grant joy, the whole share of joy that is allotted to this world. Whenever one acts against the church, one acts against joy.

Do I stop you from calculating the movement of the equinoxes or from splitting the atom? But what would it profit you to manufacture life itself if you've lost the meaning of life? All you'd have left to do would be to blow your brains out over your test tubes. Manufacture life all you want! The image you give of death is gradually poisoning the thoughts of the poor, it casts a shadow and slowly drains the colour from their last joys. It'll keep going as long as your industry and your capital allow you to turn the world into a fairground, with machines that go round at dizzying speeds, brass bands blaring, fireworks going off. But wait, just wait for the first quarter of an hour of silence. Then they will hear the word—not the one they rejected, the one that said quietly: I am the Way, the Truth and the Life—no, the one that rises from the abyss: 'I am the door forever closed, the road that leads nowhere, I am untruth and perdition.'

'I find that fascinating,' Jutta will say in contradiction to the editor, who claims that Bernanos has nothing to do with Christian tantra, assuming such a thing even exists. 'No, I think it's really good.'

The criticism of consumerism would appeal to her husband too.

For her husband's sake, because she saw that the weekend trips kept being postponed, each time for a different reason, and that first morning they took off wasn't followed by a second, because she saw that he was starting to content himself with what he had in her and what their marriage evidently no longer offered, because she wanted to see him happy—happy with her—she did her own reading about Indian religiosity, of which the workshop had given an insufficient or even entirely false impression. But not only for his sake: she herself longed to recapture the ecstasies they once shared so often—and not only the ecstasies but also the other breaks they would take, like going dancing together, to a concert or the like, having breakfast at a cafe and immersing themselves in the papers, or just being greeted with flowers. All that remained of those things were reminiscences, a joint walk here and a trip to the cinema at seven there, because the babysitter had to go to school the next morning; dinner with colleagues every few months to maintain the illusion of a private life, and then all they talked about was health insurance and maybe the children, if instead of colleagues the guests were fellow parents serving as friends. They certainly didn't talk about political commitment now that the days consisted only of work, domestic chores and his sports activities, which he used to kill the time that was left over. She fought the constant fatigue, the temptation to go to bed even before the ten o'clock news, which he found almost as stuffy as jealousy no matter how early he had to get up the next day, and was no longer prepared to accept spending the weekends alone with the children because he was on duty, or weekends on duty while he was with the children. And what they did in bed after keeping themselves awake for so long, or if he didn't reach for a book after the ten o'clock news for a change, really couldn't be called lovemaking any more.

Her agreement to buy the practice that her parents had found was also connected to the prospect of grandparents who would take the children for a weekend. What attracted him most, on the other hand, was the prospect of living in the country, even if it was just the Central German Uplands. Today she thinks it might have been better to let things take their course in the same way they did for many married couples they knew: still living in the big city and still young, they could both have found different, more suitable partners. But every time she feels so bloody lonely with her 30 appointments a day, unloved, misunderstood, unseen, she thinks of the children, just as she did whenever she imagined the concrete reality of separating—and she can never think of anything unforgivable, any more than she could back then, for if she looks at things calmly, he's not the monster she makes of him when she's in a rage; and today she also knows what followed the divorces among her acquaintances: not a different, more suitable life. Though Jutta's marriage could just as easily serve as proof that they made the right decision in spite of everything.

When Jutta's husband loads the dishwasher, a brand new device with a special flat tray for the cutlery so that more plates fit in down below, he starts by taking out everything Jutta put in the wrong way. He doesn't mention it, but of course she notices when she puts the clean dishes in the cupboard that every plate is exactly where the manufacturer intended it to be, depending on size and capacity, whether it's curved or flat; every tall glass and every low cup, all the cutlery and the long wooden spoons, meat knives or soup ladles; and every gap in the bottom rack has been used for a further glass or egg cup, though the egg cups can't be inserted just anywhere on the bottom rack, otherwise it'll slip through the rods at the bottom, and whenever someone has eaten eggs, Jutta's husband arranges the plates in such a way that there's a free gap for the egg cup right above one of the rods. If need be, he'll even take out the dirty dishes that he put in himself so he can position the egg cups. And of course the one who loves eggs is Jutta; her husband is practically a vegan.

She admits that one can fit at least 25 per cent more dishes in the washer when her husband loads it, maybe twice as many. Although it's specifically designed for pots, Jutta has stopped putting them in because she knows that her husband would take them out again and clean them by hand, as he thinks it's a waste of space. And the washing temperature would have to be set to 65 degrees rather than 55, or with less dirty dishes even 45, for the pots in the dishwasher to be clean, so it would use more electricity too. She can't help laughing when she thinks that the arguments at the squat were about no one doing the dishes, yet now she's getting worked up because her husband is so pedantic about it. He's not entirely wrong when he says that if she lived alone, she'd throw the dishes in there the same way she does with her shoes—not the glasses, of course, but certainly the cutlery. There's no need to push the spoons, forks and knives between the rods anyway, she says, as if expecting it to be as important to me as it is to her. They get just as clean when you just lay them on the cutlery tray, she's tried it secretly.

'Secretly?' I ask. 'You seriously load the dishwasher in secret because you're scared of your husband?'

'Secretly' is the wrong word for it, Jutta assures me; she just means that once, when her husband wasn't there—not because he would have had a go at her, but because he would have put the cutlery in the slots without saying anything.

'You know nothing of life,' the countess barks at the country priest. 'Oh, you priests have a naive, absurd idea of family life. It's enough,' she laughs bitterly, 'to hear you at funerals. A united family, a respected father, an incomparable mother, a consoling spectacle, the social unit, our dear France and so forth . . . The strange thing is not that you say these things, but that you imagine they move people, that you say them with pleasure. The family, monsieur . . . ' She breaks off, so abruptly that she seems literally to swallow her words.

The priest is amazed and wonders: is this the same gentle, reserved woman he had seen on his first visit to the chateau, huddled in her big armchair, her face pensive beneath the black lace? Even her voice seems to have changed, it becomes shrill, dragging on the final syllables of words when she realizes her inability to control herself. The priest has no idea how to react to the furious outburst of a woman who has previously seemed like the soul of self-restraint; indeed, the discrepancy between the peaceful house and her frightful tirades causes him such inner turmoil that he begins to stammer himself.

On leaving, he asks the countess if her husband is right. In the novel I am writing, it won't matter what the particular situation is, what matters is this: does she think her husband is right? The countess throws her head back, and the confession rises like a flash from her implacable soul: her eyes, caught in a lie, say 'yes', while her irresistible inner stirrings propel a 'no' from her half-open mouth. But here Bernanos slips up—or fine, he doesn't slip up, but he describes something else, something that's easier to understand: in this passage, the woman wants to say 'yes', but realizes she has been caught in a lie and involuntarily shouts 'no' at her marriage, at what has become of her life. It would be more complicated and opaque the other way around, and thus closer to our experience, or mine at least: the countess would have to lie with a 'no' but blurt out a 'yes', like a flash from an implacable soul, at her marriage, at what has become of her life. And then the words of the country priest would still be true:

> Of all hate, hate within the family is the most dangerous, for it cannot be assuaged at once, but in a perpetual conflict of coexistence. It is like an open abscess that poisons slowly and without fever.

'He used to be so dashing.' Jutta can't think of a different word at that moment.

I keep quiet so that she can continue in her own time.

So full of surprises, and so funny, a real scream, silly, he baffled her every day at first. He wasn't so gruff; disciplined, yes, but not averse to the odd lie-in. He was insecure, really shy, especially at first. His colleagues and the people at the community centre loved him, everyone loved him; he could be so suave, not like a stiff German, despite having a very German accent—he had no qualms about singing Paco de Lucía with that accent, with the *ay* coming out like the German for 'egg', without the consonant at the end that the flamenco singers revel in, *ayyy*, but a short *ei* like an egg. Yes, such a scream, especially on the veranda in the evenings, when the colleagues heard his egg: *Ei gran Amor, Ei tus ojos cerrados*—he played with it too. Once he leapt up, put the guitar down and danced with fingers snapping and shoes clopping, except with a thin *Ei ei ei* like a housewife at the oven rather than a trembling *ayyyyayyyyayyy*, everyone was rolling on the floor laughing. He was tender too. They had fun, real fun, it wasn't just the sex. Today she often finds him so bitter, so hard— on himself too. She finds him truly insufferable at times with his constant smart-aleckery. He didn't use to be like that, and she asks herself, if that's the distance a character covers in 25 years, from the end of youth to the start of old age, which they are both approaching at a brisk pace, if the person he has become, at her side, the person she ultimately made him too, if one becomes like that in 25 years, so dour and self-righteous, dogmatic and humourless that one can't even smile about the cereal bowl that's been left half full on the coffee table for the 85th time, my God,

and starts an argument because of a cereal bowl, just imagine
that—or was it bags of crisps today? That's right, today it was
the three started bags of crisps that he got worked up about—
when 25 years ago he got worked up about imperialism and the
exploitation of the Third World. Oh, now she's being unfair, she
knows it, but wasn't it true? Hadn't they argued about weightier
issues? About God, they spent hours arguing about God, whom
he denied and she felt, about books they had read together and
especially about politics, because he was always too far to the left
for her and he found her naive, not to mention too forgiving
towards his and her parents, who saw him as an enemy of the
constitution yet were simultaneously proud of his selflessness,
the fact that he was treating Indigenous people instead of pursuing a career, contenting himself with a room that would barely
pass as a prison cell in Germany. And the quarrels with her, back
then they were still about something, he was single-minded there
too, always had a mission, whereas today he puts solar panels on
his roof or shows off his electric car, which can't even get him to
the next big city, but he doesn't want to go there anyway, no,
doesn't want to go anywhere any more, just feels more contempt
for humanity by the year because it doesn't care about his
insights—oh God, now she's being unfair again—no, he still
makes an effort, only last year he took two weeks off to treat
refugees in Turkey, who else does that? But he could've taken
some time off for her, the kids were old enough for them to take
a trip somewhere, it doesn't have to be a romantic hotel, it's not
about luxury for her, it's about the commonality that they've lost,
discover something together again instead of spending every
holiday hiking in the mountains, where she only sees him from

the back because he's too fast, but that'd never occur to him now, the two of them, he'd only have to hold her in his arms, just pay attention to her—although, and now she's being unfair again, it's like an illness that she compulsively sees his negative sides even though she knows he's right, yes, he took the load off her when she was writing her PhD, he made sacrifices when she had cancer, yes, cancer, detected early, thank God, stood by her for months, but all she sees is just that one afternoon when he didn't cancel his appointments although her father had died, sees his two affairs but not how quickly they were over—within days, hours, only really two flirts, she tells herself, laughable really, and she says that really he's full of warmth, that he's good, just not to her so often now, or doesn't show it so often, it seems more like he's married to his children, he always thought marriage was outdated and togetherness was so reactionary that he even finds it hard to hold hands on holiday, but when does she show it? But why should she, and how, when he doesn't even want to come along to a dinner that's really important for her election chances, and he apparently doesn't care if the men stare at her, these plump, well-fed men she sat among as the only woman at the Lions Club, with their saucy jokes that naturally had nothing at all to do with the Lady Mayor, after all, the Lady Mayor can take a joke; when she sees them, not necessarily older than her husband, when she sees those fat pigs with their gilded arses and new SUVs in the gourmet restaurant's car park having their fourth course and discussing how to share 2,000 euros so that the evening will be tax-deductible, or pretending to be eternally young in their white convertibles, who have to be convinced with all manner of reasoning just to see if there's a trainee vacancy for the new Afghans, and if the Lady Mayor begs hard enough, she still gets such stupid comments—Germany simply can't take in all the weary and heavy-laden, and who's to say there aren't any terrorists among them?—the arguments she has to listen to, the level she has to stoop to just so those lard-arses will toss a few coins her way for some second-hand bikes that the local charity wants to buy, yes, there's actually one in this town, and for the schoolbooks and sneakers and medical bills and toys that the welfare office still refuses to cover despite all the applications at the national level, though her husband always does it for free, illegally if need be, but if even the Lady Mayor turns a blind eye because she sees that it's the only way—no, he still does all that, he does it for other people, with the children too, he's still always funny and dashing, in his way, he trusts them to handle things, far more than she does, and the children love him, they're proud to have a dad like that, they go cycling or hiking in the mountains together, which she doesn't usually have an appetite for or just the time, because every long weekend is destroyed by at least one appointment that she can't cancel; no, the children wouldn't find him dogmatic, dour or humourless, and the patients are full of praise too, so why does he act like that towards her now, is it just towards her? The same way she's become so bureaucratic, but only towards him, if she thinks about it, so quick to flare up and offended over nothing, and, without ever voicing it, without even believing it herself as someone with medical training, nonetheless holding him partly responsible for her illness, no, nothing left of it know, everything's OK, just some checks now, while the whole town praises her for her charm and she can hope for an absolute majority at the next election. They're not good for each other, no, neither of them, she's not good for him and he's not good for her.

Then I walk around the coffee table and finally give Jutta a hug.

Kneeling next to her armchair, I gently stroke Jutta's head, which she has laid on my shoulder. Although I'm worried that her husband will enter the living room, it's out of the question for me to end the embrace myself; I have to wait until Jutta has calmed down and lifts her head again. I'm fine now, she'll probably say, thank me or assure that she's glad we met up again, she'll get out a handkerchief or use a sleeve, or the ball of her hand, to dry her eyes just enough and wipe away the mascara, which will no doubt be smudged. Then she'll stretch her lips into her bravest smile, and her eyes while shine a little from two little slits in spite of everything. She's never looked at me like that before; she's smiled at me, of course, but not with this tear-stained gaze—and yet I know this look on her face, I can see it in my mind like a photo as I feel the growing moisture on my right shoulder. I know it from my ex-wife, exactly the same look, conveying both melancholy and an effort not to let things get her down, thanking me for the consolation while apologizing for the feelings that erupted involuntarily, I know it from other faces too, from the television, the cinema. I suddenly think of that movement of her shoe when she drew her calf towards her bottom while both turning and bending her upper body, the way she held the heel and lifted her foot out of the equally elegant shoe, then threw her calf forwards as nimbly as a dancer to send the shoe flying off her foot. As characteristic of Jutta as I found that movement, as convincingly as it expressed the same assured femininity that had knocked me for six as a 15-year-old, it was not until that evening, despite or perhaps because of her unmistakable aging, that it seemed complete; I knew the movement from somewhere and will think that the reader can visualize it too—not because they find it described so well in the novel, but because they also know that movement from somewhere. The movement doesn't belong to Jutta, to Jutta alone.

Milan Kundera, who continued the French tradition of examining love most convincingly, despite being a foreigner, developed an entire novel from a female gesture that, however characteristic, singular and also enchanting it seems at first, is something the novelist has often seen: '[ . . . ] she turned her head back towards him, smiled and lifted her right arm in the air, easily, flowingly, as if she were tossing a brightly coloured ball.' The novelist feels a pang in his heart when he sees an older lady, waving to the pool attendant as she looks back at him after the swimming lesson and walks towards the changing rooms, make exactly the same gesture that belongs to a young woman; for he wonders whether a human being might not be a unique, unrepeatable creature after all if a gesture that he identifies with one particular person, a gesture that characterizes this person and is part of their special charm, can simultaneously belong to another person. This leads him to the following reflection:

If our planet has seen some eighty billion people it is difficult to suppose that every individual has had his or her own repertoire of gestures. Arithmetically, it is simply impossible. Without the slightest doubt, there are far fewer gestures in the world than there are individuals. That finding leads us to a shocking conclusion: a gesture is more individual than an individual.

I am kneeling beside a woman of around 50 whose head is resting on my shoulder, a woman who was once my great love but is married to another man—unhappily married, I have to conclude after everything she has told me, yet she undoubtedly loves him, even if she often feels the opposite, she loves him, no question about it, and he definitely loves her; it's one of the strangest, most baffling, most emotionally conflicting situations in my life, and yet other men before me must have found themselves in exactly the same posture, consoling a beloved who is unhappily in love with another man, and they will have had the same painful and nonsensical hypotheses racing through their minds, the what-ifs that ruin our memory and the maybe-after-alls that distance us from the present; nor does the tearful smile that Jutta will no doubt show me in a moment, or the stiletto she tossed from her foot, belong to her alone.

A gesture cannot be regarded as the expression of an individual, as his creation (because no individual is capable of creating a fully original gesture, belonging to nobody else), nor can it even be regarded as that person's instrument; on the contrary, it is gestures that use us as their instruments, as their bearers and incarnations.

Isn't that equally true of our feelings and experiences? The fact that we recognize them in novels written a 100 or 200 years ago would be inexplicable otherwise. It's not only comforting, it doesn't just touch us; no, it flatters us, at least unconsciously, when we stumble on a sentence or description of a soul state in Balzac or Proust that seems to apply to us alone, expressing our own sentiment and perspective. Small personal matters are almost elevated to something universal. We find cheap replicas of the same feelings and experiences in glossy magazines, of course, which wounds our egos deeply. What seems so special to us, our innermost being and most affecting experience, is not ennobled into a universal, but turns out to be rather ordinary. The shocking thing about the marriage counselling my wife and I went through in vain—I bet Jutta and her husband have also had some counselling, or at least consultation or mediation, it's almost standard for middle- and upper-class marriages—was not the result. We'd both expected to reach the conclusion that our marriage was beyond repair (and maybe that fact was a reason for the failure the counsellor sold us as a solution). What was more shocking was that even our secret desires and most intimate experiences, the subject of our expectations and disappointments, our sexual attempts, the constant misunderstandings because we took one and the same statement to mean two totally different things, and generally the disastrous form our communication took; the habits of that bothered my wife about me and the traits that bothered me about her, her self-pity and my self-righteousness, her sentimentality and my constant striving to be rational when it's not about reason, our obstinacy and above all the hurtful things we stooped to saying, despite generally thinking we were reasonably decent people, our lovelessness, which each of us attributed to the lovelessness of the other—the fact that almost every facet of our marriage was routine for the counsellor and appeared as case studies in the books she gave us to read. Even the litany Jutta has been delivering all evening, the way she catches herself being unfair, or paints her husband as the sole culprit who simply wasn't able to appreciate her pure feelings, no wonder she protected herself with coldness; all the accusations she levelled, that he wasn't affectionate any more, they had nothing left in common, all the creativity they showed in trying to preserve their desire somehow, and that he was only loving towards the children, had become so dogmatic and such a know-it-all and was not her youthful hero any more, you don't say—those were things my wife could have said about me, some of them almost her exact words. And then Jutta, who takes her individualism as far as Christian tantrism, a form of sexuality far more sophisticated than feeding, objectophilia or cultural sodomy, decides to close the gap in her teeth, the very thing that had made her stand out from eighty billion people.

My hand, gently stroking her head, could run through her hair. It would be a signal, but innocuous enough for the embrace to remain merely a friendly or brotherly one if she lifted her head and said it was fine now. As if she hadn't noticed the announcement that would certainly be implicit in my gesture, she could still thank me for comforting her or assure me that she's glad we met up again. But if her head remained on my shoulder, my hand would glide down once her thinking time was over and brush her hairline against the grain; the tingling she would feel would be all the more pleasant because the nape of her neck is almost entirely shaved below her chin-length hair. I probe the hollow above the uppermost neck vertebra with particular care, then exploring the rest of her neck from there.

Even now, she could still lean back without more than a momentary disturbance remaining, too minor to mention, especially as I began the movement sufficiently firmly for it to pass as wholesome; after all, her neck will genuinely be stiff from the agitation and from sitting for so long. And I know a little bit about massages, I would say, though only the conventional kind; and then she'd put on her condescending smirk again and I'd smile mischievously like a little boy.

But if her head stayed there, the five fingers of my other hand, the left, which had previously been holding her back motionlessly, would begin gliding back and forth along her dress. My right hand would now touch her neck with unambiguous tenderness, advancing to places, such as the side of the neck or the area almost under her cheekbone, that are less orthopedically relevant. My left hand would join in so that her head would not feel neglected, while the right, the more experienced one, would slide down her back and then under . . . no, she would definitely feel that slipping my hand under her dress was overstepping a boundary; it could speed things up, but it could equally give her a reason to lift her head so late that it would no longer be possible to end the embrace on an enjoyable note. On her dress, then, on her dress—my right hand would land on her dress and stroke her back and both her sides through the fabric, yes, would already move frontwards and encroachingly into her armpit, where there is sadly no opening, as the dress is not sleeveless, while the second hand, the left, would now also slide down to press her body closer to mine. One of the two hands would ultimately probe further downwards, probably the second hand, the left, so that the right would assert its position at the side, near her breast; the left would pause on her hip to give her some final thinking time, and would then land, fingers spread, on her bottom.

Now, at the latest, she would have to react, would either have to throw her arms around me so that our mouths would soon search for each other, or pull her upper body back and then probably get up. Not reacting would be a clear consent for me to unabashedly touch her breasts, ardently grab her buttocks and soon reach into the gap between the armchair and her bottom to move my hand even further forwards. But she probably wouldn't sit there so passively, that wouldn't be like her. She would make a choice as the two hypotheses were now, at the latest, racing through her mind too.

Whether we read the book or not, we all—or rather, the men among us—grew up with Thérèse Raquin (and Anna Karenina, Werther's Lotte and so forth in other literatures), that is, the dream of a woman whom we release from the prison of her marriage to live with her wildly and dangerously, as it said on the postcards in our school days: 'Her hungry body threw itself into the experience of pleasure with total abandon,' Zola writes of his Thérèse: 'She was emerging from a dream and awakening into passion.' And the women—readers or not, since the early evening serials are also based on literary tradition, and their triviality lies not in the motifs themselves but in the fact that they repeat them to the point of senselessness—the women, even in old age, still carry with them the image of a man who will love them unreservedly, not according to the rules. It makes no difference that Marguerite is the luxury-spoilt mistress and Armand the young man from a respectable family; this inversion of social roles only makes Dumas's *Camille* even more exquisite. What matters is that the lover finally bursts into the captive lady's room to throw himself at her feet, then covers her hands in tears of passion and exclaims:

> My life belongs to you, Marguerite, what do you need this man for when you have me? How could I ever leave you, and how I repay you for the happiness you give me? There is no longer anything constraining us, my Marguerite, we love each other! What do the others matter to us?

Indeed, all these novels end tragically: in Goethe the lover kills himself, in Tolstoy the wife does so and in Zola the two of them kill the husband together. Until the sexual revolution, literature was certainly not arguing the case for adultery. Nonetheless, it didn't simply warn the reader; Zola, Tolstoy, Goethe and the rest also gave voice to a longing and thus planted an expectation in us that, rightly or wrongly, eats away at bourgeois marriage. It is Camille, of all people, who stands outside of bourgeois society: she silently endures the pain of separation and even the desperate contempt of her lover, who is ignorant of the selfless motive for her retreat.

For 30 years I've imagined the tenderness that is now within my reach; I would only have to bend the fingers of my right hand as they stroke her head, and the friendly gesture would turn into a caress that she would either reject or allow to happen. Either way, she would have made her decision again 30 years later. Why don't I try it? The fact that she didn't sit up promptly when I knelt down next to her and guided her head towards my shoulder is probably itself a signal that she welcomes the tenderness, even expects it. No, I'm no longer the insecure boy and she's no longer the near-grown woman. I was at first, when Jutta approached me at the book table, but more out of bafflement than the inability to deal with it. Jutta poured her heart out to me, I didn't, she drank too much, I didn't, has already smoked two joints, bitched about her husband and talked about their sexual practices, cried, repeated herself and tried to impress me by slagging off the Lions Club, not realizing how boundless her self-pity is. She barely knows more about me than what's in the novel, and maybe only the passages I read last night; I'm not going to ask her if she insists on keeping quiet about her reading experience. I'm sure it wasn't just the name I gave her in the novel that bothered her; also the fact that I made our love out to be bigger than it probably was from her perspective. But who's to say that I'm the same as the 'I' in the novel—the one I wrote and the one I will write. This evening she barely learnt more about me than the fact that I'm a good listener, which is part of my job; politicians are evidently more used to speaking.

What's stopping me from bending the fingers of my right hand and running them through her hair? It's not the famous dilemma faced by Swann, who won Odette the moment he stopped loving her—won her because he stopped loving her, or stopped loving her because he won her. Despite the unappealing expression that Jutta's face can assume, like any other, I still consider her an enchanting woman and imagine how a life with her might have turned out—or might still turn out. The way she feels so sorry for herself, well, we've all been guilty of that. The same way she keeps the publisher of the local paper on side, I pay the literary critic a compliment. We generally forgive our beloved for everything, and the fading of love could be defined by the fact that more and more things bother us. As if I love her! The very word points to the next flight of fancy. As if what a 15-year-old feels towards a girl for a week could be love. But I find her appealing, even if my desire is only so great because its fulfilment would come after 30 years of expectation. And then she spoke with such promise about sex, and believes that every person—which would include me—is capable of an ecstasy that I previously only found hinted at in medieval treatises. Sure, what I'd like most would be to tear her clothes off. It's not fear that keeps me from even feeling her hair. As I say, I'd hardly be risking anything—or at most, risk her husband entering the room or one of the kids, which would be worse, and she'd have this danger in mind, I assume; despite all the passion I am imagining, she would still pay attention to the stairs in case someone was coming down, or to the light switch, which one can hear clicking from the living room because it has an energy-saving switch-off function. Nor is it a concern that once satisfied, my longing would turn into regret. One knows things like that from reading about them in books, but one doesn't learn from it.

No, it's something else: while I desire her, or at least her body, I'm also thinking of the novel, which—as I now know—will not be about our love. If an affair developed now, or even more than an affair, as improbable as that may seem, namely a relationship, I'd no longer be neutral enough to write about her marriage—to be willing, able or entitled to do so. However calculating I may be, I'm not the kind of arsehole one has to be for literature to take all available liberties. Or rather: I am, I could be, if it weren't for Jutta. Whatever her name is, she has a name that will be written on her grave. What the novelist will present as self-pity only shows me how desperate she is—or drunk?— if someone who comes across as so strong and self-confident can still indulge in maudlin behaviour. She'll find it embarrassing, or already does, as she seems to have calmed down in my arms. Maybe she would actually be happier with me; the simple fact that we wouldn't have to carry a twenty-year marriage around with us, twenty years of daily routine, twenty years that would have worn down even the truest love, twenty years full of reproaches, not one of them ever forgotten, while the other's positive qualities, their faithfulness, their loyalty, drift down into the unconscious, assuming they don't just disappear into thin air; twenty years of misunderstandings, constantly renewed reconciliations, unfulfilled, unfulfillable longings and the disappointment that, although it extends to everything except perhaps the children, we blame on our husband, our wife, because life itself offers no answer.

Kneeling next to her armchair, I indecisively stroke Jutta's head, which she has laid on my shoulder. My gaze wanders across the third of the room that I can see from this angle: at the left edge of my field of view part of the bookshelf, opposite me the dark glass front that opens onto the terrace, in front of that the reading chair, which revolves so that one can enjoy the view at the same time, in the corner the barbell, which is evidently lifted by Jutta's husband, no pictures on the walls, which I actually like, and the decor is generally sparing and almost as impersonal as in a furnished apartment, albeit one that's also inhabited by children;

DVD boxes, open bags of crisps, a board game and the football jersey are strewn across the stone floor and the carpet, with the electric guitar leaning against the amplifier. Or is it the father who plays that, having returned to more youthful music after Paco de Lucía?

'Refuge for the Homeless' is the title of the section that contains the most famous line from *Minima Moralia*. Here, Adorno not only rejects as intolerable the traditional living rooms of the bourgeois family, that stuffy cosiness in which Jutta and I were the last generation to grow up; as early as 1948, he was already railing against the new functional furnishings: as a result of the cost-reducing possibility of self-assembly, the marketing principle on which furniture chains rely, they wiped the slate clean in even the most provincial areas. They are 'designed by experts for philistines, or factory sites that have strayed into the consumption sphere,' Adorno inveighs, 'devoid of all relation to the occupant: in them even the nostalgia for independent existence, defunct in any case, is sent packing.' In fact, he asserts, one cannot even dwell at all any more; those who buy more stylish residences are embalming themselves alive. As ever, the ones who cannot choose have it the worst: 'They live, if not in slums, in bungalows that by tomorrow may be leaf-huts, trailers, cars, camps or the open air.' No individual can stop the end of the bourgeois lifestyle; as soon as they occupy themselves with furniture design and interior decoration, they find themselves in proximity to 'the arty-crafty sensibilities of the bibliophile'. In such a situation, it seems a wise choice to evade residential responsibility by moving like an exile into a hotel or furnished apartment—or so one might think if one is not forced into exile. 'The best mode of conduct, in face of all this, still seems an uncommitted, suspended one: to lead a private life, as far as the social order and one's own needs will tolerate nothing else, but not to attach weight to it as to something still socially substantial and individually appropriate.'

It's interesting that Adorno moves seamlessly from living room furnishings to private life in general. Perhaps there's an encouraging, even hopeful message in there for Jutta and her husband; at any rate, it's precisely the air of something borrowed, something hastily put together that I like about the decor. It's rare enough with Jutta's middle-class background, certainly rarer than her career development, place of residence and profession, her views, sexual preferences and marital problems, that the living room doesn't desperately attempt some kind of aesthetic self-definition, which would simply be limited to choosing between different furniture catalogues anyway. The walls don't look as if they were left white for the sake of the composition, but out of indifference.

> But the thesis of this paradox leads to destruction, a loveless disregard for things which necessarily turns against people too; and the antithesis, no sooner uttered, is an ideology for those wishing with a bad conscience to keep what they have. Wrong life cannot be lived rightly.

And if her fingers, pressed against my chest, started moving? I should consider in advance how to react so that situation, however unlikely it may be, to avoid leaving her in any state of uncertainty. If she already had her arm wrapped around my neck, it would be humiliating if I rejected her—so much more humiliating than vice versa. If I stroked her now, if I initiated the tenderness, I would simply be doing what's natural for a man and what a lover is expected to do when he finally holds the beauty in his arms. She, on the other hand—and this would be obvious to both of us—would not surrender to me because I meant a great deal to her; she would surrender to me because her marriage no longer meant anything, because she didn't want it to mean anything. There might be some desire involved, a desire aroused by the rapid intimacy that felt so good to both of us, and which had evidently become so rare for Jutta, by the understanding she found in me, maybe also by her image of me as a poet and thus some kind of anti-bourgeois metropolitan globetrotter, perhaps that's really how she imagines me, without knowing—without being able to know, as I haven't said a word about it—what my daily routine actually looks like, a desire further encouraged by the cocktail of overexhaustion and soft drugs as well as the simple fact of two sexually compatible people spending several hours in the same room and experiencing it as somehow significant; a desire she may not even have realized a few minutes earlier, and would come to light all the more surprisingly in this direct physical closeness that has already lasted for seconds. And yet: desire alone would never overcome her morals, nor—despite the energy-saving light switch—her fear of snogging with a stranger in her own living room when her husband or even one of her children could walk through the door at any moment. Even when the bishop revealed his feelings to her at their reunion, she didn't breathe a word about her own infatuation.

No, someone like Jutta wouldn't jeopardize her marriage—no, not just her marriage, a whole family—for the sake of a fleeting attraction. It would be exactly the other way around: she would be succumbing to the attraction in order to jeopardize her marriage and even her family. She would have lost everything if her mouth sought a kiss and I didn't take her. So much more would be at stake if her fingers moved now, so much more than for me: not just one life, but a fabric of different lives. Maybe it would be right to break it up, maybe it would be wrong. Either way, I'd have to decide before she wrapped her arm around my neck, would have to return her affection or change my position as if by coincidence, as if kneeling had become too tiring, and smile at her in an emphatically platonic and cheering way. I'd either have to love her or pretend I hadn't noticed her gesture, otherwise the relationship—which is more than a professional one for me—would inevitably be destroyed.

When I write the novel, I won't only browse French literature. I'll also listen to music that has nothing to do with Jutta, that definitely isn't her kind of music and therefore won't be woven into the plot to begin with, unlike the books on her shelf. The reader might think that I'm still a fan of Neil Young, whom I surely wouldn't have mentioned twice already just by chance; but that book about Neil Young was half an eternity ago, and meanwhile I've practically caught up with Bloch in *Lost Time* by outdoing all the natives in my love for the classical tradition, my word. Yes, Debussy too, whom Proust calls Vinteuil because he was reluctant to use real names, yes, I know Debussy well enough to imagine him in the CD rack standing next to Jutta's bookshelf like a pot plant. My God, that CD rack really is ghastly, I've only just noticed it, but it also occurs to me that Debussy goes perfectly with her reading, which maybe I'll only imagine when I write the novel, because the illumination of the psychology of bourgeois love in the French literature of the nineteenth and early twentieth century still applies today. But the reader, as ever, would be right: thanks to a turn of events that seems too contrived for any novelist to venture, I will actually return to Neil Young, I'll keep returning to the same long piece as I sit at the desk, or often don't sit any more but get up to absorb it with my body—not dancing, simply swaying my upper body back and forth to get into the rhythm, which isn't fast, never fast, and only speeds up sometimes like in an argument or some quick sex, but then goes back into the familiar plod; it's tired yet steady, like a long drive, a drive on the motorway, and feeling the bass, that thick, fat, unbelievably powerful bass, which is a fundamental tone for me, a fundamental tone for life itself, simultaneously frightening because it's so powerful, one can never miss it even for a second—dum dumdum, dum dumdum—the same three rumbling notes time and time again over the drums, which push on stubbornly, and in between them the two guitars like a married couple, a married couple whose partners speak to each other or don't, communicating silently most of the time, their thoughts speaking to each other during the long drive; except that in real life, the lead guitar is not always the same, at least not in Jutta's marriage and not in mine either, maybe not in any love, if it is love. Such beautiful, such poignant music.

Twenty years of fidelity. Twenty years, and they still get worked up about each other. Twenty years in which they were there for each other when it mattered more than it does for a dinner or even when there are tears in bed. He was in bed in the jungle with a temperature of 40.5 degrees, and she stood next to him, taking away his fear. She fell out with her boss, and he said: 'Fuck him, I'll earn the money for now so that you can finish your PhD. I'll go everywhere with you.' Twenty years in which they built up three lives together. Twenty years in which he went through depression for three years, clinical depression, and she endured his indifference, his pessimism and fatigue without a word of complaint, taking the load off his back during all his rehab and treatment. Twenty years, but the summer holidays were usually enjoyable and passed with almost no quarrelling. Twenty years in which she had cancer and he spent days, weeks finding the right therapy, the best clinic, practically alerting the whole of German oncology even though the diagnosis wasn't actually that dramatic. Twenty years in which he wiped up her vomit cheerfully, with a smile, when it all suddenly erupted from her during chemotherapy, the urine, even the faeces with a smile. Unbelievable: malaria, depression, cancer, all in twenty years, and how soon one forgets the illnesses again. Twenty years, and her father isn't there any more. Twenty years in which she tried to forgive him for two affairs. Twenty years in which three children were conceived, born, cradled in their arms, brought up. Twenty years with two puberties, and the youngest is practically going through it already. Twenty years in which two people saw all of each other, all the embarrassing things. He led them to a circle of chairs with naked strangers, while she burst into tears at a fete and threw pasta salad out of jealousy. Twenty years in which he trusted her when she took up tantra seriously. Twenty years, and they still enjoyed making love. Twenty years with her hysteria, escalating from the most trivial causes, twenty years with his stupid jokes that no one except him laughs about.

Twenty years in which he had to accept that he was now a German country doctor and she had to accept that she hadn't married a film hero. Twenty years in which each followed through the mirror of the other how their own body was being used up, line by line, wrinkle by wrinkle, and even his sporting activities didn't really help. Twenty years of his and her smell. Twenty years of snoring, or when exactly did the snoring start? Twenty years in which they constantly argued about parenting, although they knew that he was a good father and she a good mother. Twenty years in which neither of them ever doubted the other's goodness, though certainly plenty of other things—love, understanding, his fidelity and her honesty, but not that they were good. twenty years in which he still hadn't learnt to pronounce the Spanish *ay* but there's no singing she likes better. Twenty years in which their books gradually covered the living room wall.

'Twenty-three years,' Jutta will correct me.

A life told in a few minutes, a night, a novel, is like the film that famously passes before one's eyes when in fear of death. It usually only lasts two seconds, three or four at most, but it feels endless to you because you see so many pictures in succession, scenes, conversations or at least fragments of conversations, from childhood and from yesterday. When one meets a lover again and she tries to recount 30 years, it's like that flash of images. Then life seems to consist only of events, and becomes as deceptive as a novel, for the events may be the least important thing of all. Even the birth of a child only takes place on one day, but you live with that child day after day. It's the same child, the same miracle, the same trembling that would seize you out of happiness and worry if your attention hadn't necessarily been worn down. Even love: so much harder to notice it in one's daily routine than after a rendezvous. 'Theoretically we are aware that the earth is spinning, but in reality we do not notice it,' Proust writes:

> To make its passing perceptible, novelists have to turn the hands of the clock at dizzying speed, to make the reader live through ten, twenty, thirty years in two minutes. At the top of a page, we have been with a lover full of hope; at the foot of the following one, we see him again, already an octogenarian, hobbling his painful daily way round the courtyard of an old people's home, barely acknowledging greetings, remembering nothing of his past.

I felt no fear when the tyres lost their grip and the car went flying across the icy road, between two oncoming cars, into the woods and slammed head-on into a tree. I think it was only after the collision that my heart started racing. The endlessness felt like extreme calm. And I only heard the naked sound of rock 'n' roll from the car radio again when I realized that we were alright. It was happy, that flight, genuinely happy to fly through one's own life—and how much happier to fly through someone else's life.

I feel a nagging doubt whether she really is Jutta. I'd like to have a closer look at her face. She barely said anything about the old days, barely more than she would have learnt from the book I read from tonight, didn't show any interest in correcting some detail or other—her name, sure, but nothing else. It's normal for at least the first hour of class reunions or similar counters to be spent comparing and completing shared memories, I would think. But she said and asked so little about the week of our love that I'd have to summon a great deal of willpower to keep believing it was love for her. She knows our home town, that's clear; her pietistic village, her parents, that all lines up and it's too particular to be made up. Although: come to think of it, she hasn't really said all that much about her background, and she could have picked up the little she did mention from the novel, which is at least on her bookshelf. But why would she have duped me? And she wouldn't know her real name if she weren't Jutta, who isn't really called Jutta. Now I remember: I addressed her by name when she said I shouldn't dare make the dedication to Jutta. In theory she could have started the game spontaneously when she realized I took her for Jutta, and then it developed the way it developed, and she just couldn't go back on it, or maybe she didn't want to once she saw how well I understood her, or she thought—this seems more plausible in retrospect—that I knowingly joined in with her little joke, and she didn't even take the charade seriously or think for a second about a youthful love, our love; and meanwhile I was connecting everything she was telling me about herself with the girl in the smokers' corner. But isn't that all a bit far-fetched?

I go through our conversations again in my head, but can't decide whether such an absurd mix-up is really possible. But I do notice something else: the books on the shelf—they needn't actually be hers. They could just as easily, or perhaps more likely, belong to her husband; her remarks on French literature were hardly very knowledgeable. As a mayor, she probably barely has time to read, with appointments most evenings, and saves a page-turner like *The Red and the Black* for the holidays. As far as I can tell, she only really raved about *The Memoirs of Two Young Wives*, which is really bedtime reading. The only writers on the shelf that she read at school are García Márquez, Neruda and Vargas Llosa, and only their most famous works. But her face, her face, it's very clearly her face: the colour of her eyes, the nose, more a round head than a tall one, even though she's so dainty, always has been. What bothers me more than the changes to her face, which I can attribute to age and my imprecise memory, is that she's so short, a whole head shorter than me. When I stood facing her in my mind's eye she was almost as tall as me, even if that was still a 15-year-old's mental image 30 years later. But what I don't want to believe, although I expected it, must have expected it, is that the gap in her teeth no longer exists.

The editor will complain that I have failed to make use of the central elements of suspense, despite setting them up quite skilfully. Instead of bringing Neil Young into things so late on, which is really a little pubescent, he should long since have had Jutta's husband appear—the complications that would arise just from that! Her husband could have presented his view as if speaking of a different marriage. He could have started an argument with me, or I with him, and Jutta could have demonstratively taken his side, which would be psychologically rather improbable—though what man can accurately predict the vagaries of the female psyche?—so that I would perhaps not have saved the marriage, but at least created a rare moment of harmony that would make a reconciliation conceivable, even desirable (it won't occur to the editor that Jutta could have taken my side in the argument). Or Jutta would argue with her husband herself when he entered the room, yes, she'd yell at him and throw crisp bags or the half-full cereal bowl at him again; then I'd either become the intermediary for a love so much greater than mine or convince Jutta finally to start a new life, because one shouldn't carry on when there's so little love. I could take her by the hand and save her from the raging and the blows of her husband, so that we'd end up in my hotel room after all, though without any sex. Or maybe with sex? 'A thousand possibilities!' the editor will exclaim, but instead of that, I have Jutta's head resting endlessly on my shoulder. Now, at the latest, one of the children would have to burst into the living room— what a drama that might cause: tears, explanations, declarations, or maybe just a glance, the mute, sad or helpless glance of a child, and then the door would already have shut, and the reader would hear the child running upstairs. What a drama would be going on inside of Jutta, all that inner conflict: should she run after the child, should she stay, should one continue a marriage for the children's sake?

'They're not children any more,' I will remind the editor, 'the youngest is almost 15.'

'All the better,' he will say; 'then they can speak for themselves.'

The editor will entirely forget the smartphone that's been lying on the table for hours. It could bring the most unlikely messages into the living room: a text, an email, breaking news, things that would no doubt flash up on a politician's screen. At the touch of a button, world events would enter the novel I'll write. After all, I've already set up the current affairs angle with the reference to Houellebecq—some announcement: Afghanistan, Iraq, Somalia, Jutta would immediately bring up Islam again and I'd be back to Albert Bloch, whom no degree of assimilation can help. But what am I supposed to do? No messages arrive, or at least Jutta doesn't check, neither now nor during the entire evening, doesn't seem to fit the cliche of the news-addicted politician. She glanced briefly in the phone's direction once or twice when something flashed on the screen, but didn't pick it up—or if she did, I was in the toilet at the time. Her husband probably went to bed long ago, unless he's still doing the accounts, and her children aren't going to make a scene; at that age, they have other things on their mind than the saga of their parents' marriage anyway. I kneel beside Jutta, who has laid her head on my shoulder without anything happening.

In the worst case, I would confirm her prejudices if I now bent the fingers of my right hand to run them through her hair. She would no longer see me, just me, but would suddenly, triggered by the movement of the eight smallest joints in the human body, see a background that makes her uncomfortable. And how could I deny her right to that feeling only a few weeks after the Paris attacks, which, unlike the 'Jewish invasion' of the early twentieth century, are completely real—and when she herself is the only person pushing for the mosque. Well, she'll only mention the mosque when the reads the novel I'm writing; I don't know about that yet, any more than about the 130 people that will die half a year later in Paris again, in Paris of all places. But her generation, our West German generation, grew up with female emancipation, the struggle for abortion rights and against marital rape, which still wasn't a punishable crime, for women's refuges, women's bookshops, women's representatives; so I don't need to ask her what she thinks—what she *must* think—about wives walking behind their husbands or schoolboys who don't respect teachers because they're women. And then she's a Christian too, one of those emphatically enlightened Protestants who see their own Middle Ages repeating themselves in Islam. The fact that she asks me about terror is enough for me to add all the other things she's thinking. In the worst case, she'd think that I, whom she has shown immense trust, who knows of the fragility of her marriage, and thus the whole fabric in which her family exists, that I can't deal with the situation, can't keep my urges under control, that I am exploiting her need for comfort and support for sexually-charged touching that she wasn't even thinking of when she laid her head on my shoulder, or when she leant her shoulder against my arm on the terrace before that.

Perhaps the reader—more likely the male than the female—will find my concern excessive; but one can get a little neurotic with all the things people say about the Orient, a category in which Jutta also puts me, even if she thinks or even stated expressly that I wasn't meant. Even in private, one is affected by projections that another person may not even be making simply because, however, unconsciously, one is at pains not to confirm them; one does one's best with one's liberalism, and reacts all the more sensitively to a hostility that one imputes although no one has hinted at it. That is exactly what Proust describes, and this would be the only parallel—not reality, not an actual or purported invasion, but what goes on in Albert Bloch's mind and my own. It bothers me, it really gets up my noise, that Jutta keeps suggesting I read Houellebecq, because her recommendation is not a literary but a pedagogical one.

'You still haven't read his book,' Jutta will complain, reproaching me for my own hostility.

'Sure I have,' I will respond evasively, 'but the novelist hasn't.'

Thirty years ago she didn't ask about background. Sure, she liked the dark hair, the aura of foreignness, the 'Southern' euphoria; it must have been somehow exotic. But it was never about what kind of culture it was. If anything, it was a bonus that I didn't look like everyone else. And religion was the last thing that interested us.

To annoy my editor a little more, who finally wants to know where the embrace leads, I'll return to Neil Young, even though he's at least as out of place in the novel I'm writing as he would be in the CD rack in Jutta's living room. My goodness, that CD rack! Any reader roughly my age is sure to know the type: a revolving stand, the kind they use in shops for brochures or paperback, with an—oh God!—Afro-brown, exaggeratedly slim woman's head on top that people used 20 years ago to demonstrate their liking for world music; and something like this, this death stake of open-mindedness, next to Stendhal, Proust, Balzac, Zola, Flaubert, Baudelaire and Céline as well—I would say it's far more out of place than Neil Young, let alone Houellebecq. But Neil Young: it's not only the droning bass line, the drums constantly pushing at the speed limit, the two guitars that talk and talk and talk like a man and a woman in a car, without saying more than the odd practical phrase—where are we stopping, I need a pee, when are we getting something to eat?—for over 20 minutes, an eternity for a rock song and even longer on live recordings; an eternity of nothing but thoughts circling in one's head, conflicting emotions that react to the thoughts and feelings of the other like electric oscillations, sensing them like the bass lines played by Billy Talbot, each of his three notes vibrating through the body, dum dumdum, so that one knows without asking that the other person is dwelling on similar thoughts, that their feelings are equally conflicted: is what we have together good or it is far too little, should I be grateful or is my patience making me ill, and won't I be lonely either way, with or without the other, and doesn't it come to the same thing, or shouldn't we hold onto what we do actually share? It's not only the interplay of the four instruments, the naked sound of rock 'n' roll, that always makes me think of an aging married couple on their way to or back from a holiday—no, the lyrics say it too, the few lines I can understand, it's a whole marriage saga that Neil Young is recounting with drums, bass and two guitars: so many years together, he says, all the good times, ups and downs, 'So many joys raisin' up those kids', now they've left the house, they live somewhere else; there it is, a whole existence in four lines, one that seems ordinary, a happy existence too. But at the end of the first verse, so incidentally that I only noticed it at the second or third listen, Neil young sings that she, the woman, tried so often and cried so often. That little addition, a single banal rhyme—tried/cried—transforms this marriage, however unassuming, unspectacular and outwardly harmonious, into a drama, which most marriages subjectively are. That's exactly where the chorus enters: every morning the sun rises and they wake up next to each other, carry on with whatever they were doing—and then, completely out of the blue: 'She loves him', three times, and then: 'She does what she has to', and once more, half with determination and half in despair, 'She loves him, she loves him so, she loves him so', but this time followed by 'She does what she *needs* to'.

In the second verse, the two seem to stop at a hotel, a Ramada Inn—which is the title of the song—and the mere name conjures up not just a very American hotel, but also the middle-class income needed to pay for it. They order something, 'some restaurant food and a bottle', and the phrase 'restaurant food' already makes it clear that they're not in the habit of eating out, that they're from the generation which spoke of 'restaurant food' because the women still stood at the stove, 'some restaurant food'—not Italian, Chinese or steak; because 'restaurant food' is nothing wholesome, the phrase makes it clear that it's about something else, 'feels right', it's about breaking out of their daily routine this once, hence the wine, going straight for a bottle: 'Had a few drinks and now they're feeling fine'. They're heading south to meet old friends, school friends, 'people they haven't seen forever'; they have enough time now, and one really can't tell if it's good, what they have together, or whether it's not far too little, should they be grateful or does their patience make them ill, and won't they be lonely either way, with or without the other, and doesn't it come to the same thing, or shouldn't they hold onto what they do actually share? Then the chorus again, only this time he's the one who 'loves her so' and does what he must, three times 'he loves her so' and does whatever it is that Neil Young means by 'what he needs to'.

At the end it all falls apart somehow; I can't follow all the lyrics because of the American accent and the way he sings, but it seems they've sat facing each other for a bit too long, drunk too much, they're getting on each other's nerves in the restaurant and saying nothing. He seems completely different, just looks away and 'checks out'; no idea what 'checks out' means here, it clearly doesn't refer to checking out in the sense of leaving, because he stays in his seat and she finally says they have to do something—maybe marriage counselling, is that the norm in America too?—but 'He just pulls another tall one / Closes his eyes and says "that's enough" ', and then it's the chorus again, saying that every morning, the sun rises and they wake up next to each other: 'And she loves him so', does what she needs to, and 'he loves her so', does whatever he needs to. I will ask myself every time, while the guitars join the motorway and I feel that thick, fat, unbelievably powerful bass over the drums, which push on stubbornly, what exactly is enough, what he means when he says 'that's enough', considering how they love each other in the chorus and carry on with what they've been doing.

'How late is it anyway?' Jutta asks after lifting her head.

On her face, the unchanged girl's face I imagined for 30 years, I see age like a mask that, in a moment, she will wipe away along with the tears, the crumbling layer of makeup and the mascara.

'No idea,' I reply, dropping my arms. 'My phone must still be in my coat, shall I get it?'

'No need,' says Jutta, leaning down to the knee-high table to look at her smartphone: 'It's already past five.'

Uncertain whether to sit back down on the sofa or take my leave, I stand up. Either way, I should go to the toilet first.

'I think I'll get myself to the hotel,' I say, since Jutta doesn't say any more. 'Could you call a taxi?'

'Hm, that's tricky at this hour.'

'Oh, I see.'

'This isn't the city. But I can quickly drive you there.'

'Rubbish, the fresh air will do me good.'

'It's not that far to be honest, quarter of an hour or so.'

'Alright then. Will I find it?'

'I can explain it to you, shouldn't be a problem.'

I'm not sure how to read the look on her face, which seems to contrast, though almost imperceptibly, with her friendly offer to drive me to the hotel. The word 'businesslike' comes to mind—yes, she looks businesslike with her lips pressed tightly together, her firm voice sounds businesslike with its pointedly clear articulation, and even the way she's sitting seems business-like, with her spine almost overstretched as if to be prepared for any questions; but this emphatic efficiency is almost comical at the same time, for her eyes are still tear-stained and her mascara is running down her cheeks like the tributaries of a stream. It makes me think of politicians who carry on a campaign speech with a cream pie all over their face.

'I'll get you a tissue,' I say and go to the kitchen, where I saw a roll of paper towels when Jutta was making tea.

When I return to the living room with the roll, Jutta is still sitting straight in the armchair. I walk over to her, and am just about to tear off two or three paper towels for her when she grabs my wrist.

'How early do you have to get up tomorrow?' I ask, because she's silent again.

She looks at me with such astonishment that I'm not sure if she understood the question. Two or three seconds pass like that, maybe more, in which I brace myself for an outburst, at least a second crying fit or a confession. Or a decision? But then, as if she had just gone for a quick walk in her thoughts, she returns to the living room and switches to a friendly, casual manner that I could imagine being her working mode. I expect she gives her secretary the same look when she asks her something unimportant.

'Well, normally at eight,' she says, reaching for her smartphone again, 'but I think I can make it a bit later, I'll just have a look.'

While she runs her index finger over the screen, she asks what I think about the refugees from the Balkans, by which she doesn't mean the Syrians and Afghans that will come half a year later via the Balkans, but the actual Kosovars, Albanians or Serbs themselves; evidently she's picked up some headline or the subject of an email. I admit that I don't really have an opinion and, although I really don't feel like politics at this moment, start talking about the one hand and the other.

'Here on the ground we look at things a bit differently,' Jutta counters, though it doesn't sound particularly committed. No doubt her election mode is rather different.

I'm starting to think that she's delaying my departure, consciously or not. It's obvious right now: I've already said I'm leaving, and she starts a new topic that doesn't even particularly interest her. I wonder whether it's been going on all night; I was so happy to see her again, and like the 15-year-old, took it for granted that she'd turn me away and I'd never leave her of my own accord—maybe I thought it was my God-given role to win her over, and that prevented me from noticing that Jutta was also drawing out our reunion. At any rate, unlike the film heroes, I really need the toilet now; but Jutta seems to have forgotten, as she's still holding onto my wrist, making me stand next to her look a schoolboy learning his lesson. That would be fine if it were actually a lesson, but she's just talking about a reader's letter she wrote to the *Frankfurter Allgemeine Zeitung*. Now, with her grotesquely smudged mascara, she really looks a bit like those politicians with pie on their face, except that she lacks any verve; it feels as if she's just waffling about something or other. It feels as if she's holding onto me somehow.

'But that's not even the point here!' I call out to my own surprise and pull my hand away somewhat roughly.

'What do you mean?'

'That's not the point!'

'What isn't?'

'The point is that you can't just weigh up the pros and cons, it doesn't work like that. The point is that you can't say, "here are the good sides and there are the bad sides", and then we just draw the balance.'

'I still don't understand what you mean.'

'I mean you, the two of you; I mean that you're not connected by good experiences and separated by bad experiences, it's far more complicated.'

'Well sure.'

'What binds you to your husband is your hate for him.'

'Hate?'

'Yes, hate.'

'But I don't hate him at all.'

'Yes you do, you hate him just the way my wife hated me and I hated my wife and your husband maybe hates you too, and this hate is love at the same time, one can't separate the two any more when one's lived together so long and so closely, because by hating him so much, you love him at the same time, otherwise you'd have broken up long ago, if it were just hate, but if it were just love, pure pretty love, if that even exists, then you wouldn't feel that anger towards him, that rage, and you also love him because you can throw your hate at him, because he lets you do that to him and does the same to you. Anyone else would tell you to get lost and vice versa. But you, you love each other, and that's why you hate each other too.

'Hm. Well, I think "hate" is too strong a word.'

'Then call it aggression or something.'

'I don't know; could it be that you're relying too much on your own experiences?'

'Could be.'

Before I disappear to the toilet, Jutta asks if I'm sure I don't want her to drive me; I should be honest, she insists.

I can't explain the fact that you've given me your attention over so many pages, except—I don't want to say because of love— because of some kind of folly. I keep wondering who you are, whether old or young, man or woman, married or not, even whether you're fat or thin, well read or not, and most of all: how things are with your love; I sometimes ask myself on the train or in a cafe whether you happen to know me, but at the same time shrink back from the answer, because if you did actually speak to me I'd only stammer or make some commonplace remark.

I suppose you assumed I wouldn't think about you, in keeping with the cliche of the poet as a loner who doesn't care about other people's opinions, that I'd read your warm or insulting letters indifferently and only check reviews too see if they had any good quotes for publisher to put on the paperback editions. But that's nonsense, and I think that for once, I can speak for all novelists when I say this: of course I care whether something comes back from the void into which I call out, and I'm happy if the things that matter to me, however positive or negative your judgement, means something to you, for your own life. The comparison to Stendhal that one critic made, for example, I mentioned it right at the start of the novel—it didn't make me happy because of Stendhal, but because the critic's opinion, this particular critic's opinion, means a lot *to me*. I always read his long, erudite reviews, which now only appear online because there's not enough space in the papers, and they probably don't expect their readers to be interested in something full of references to Stendhal, Proust, Balzac, Zola or Flaubert, or generally with nineteenth- or early twentieth-century literature, which is closer to me than the present—I always read your reviews, Mr Schütte, and always learn something new, admire your meticulousness, your judgement, and I always sense a political outlook too, one that, for all your loyalty to the

European tradition, is the opposite of reactionary; and I assume you do all this purely out of enthusiasm, even a strange kind of obsession, because you don't make any money from it online. And you wouldn't believe what a joy it was for me to discover that you—again, I wouldn't dare to say that you 'love' my literature—but that you follow it attentively, which is far more important, and react to it.

Of course a novelist enjoys good sales and high scores in the book tips; but if it were only about success, then they could probably find an easier way, probably everyone could, whatever their profession—even the baker who wanted to sell as many rolls as possible, the politician who only cared about votes, the editor who could rubber-stamp my manuscripts, and even in personal relationships—if one just wanted to be considered likeable. Writing a novel, writing it it seriously, I mean, immersing oneself for weeks or months in one's own reading, staring day in, day out at the blank paper or the black hole of one's computer screen, a novelist only does all that—and, as I say, I feel I can speak for others too—in the hope of finding you. The fact that the novel I will write has so many asides is not just because of a literary game; each time it's an opportunity to imagine the reader holding the novel in their hands: I don't even know you.

I stop in the hallway and look at the floor of the structure in which Jutta exists: the shoes of different sizes, the bicycle helmets, the skateboard and the basketball, which has rolled against the doctor's bag, on the dresser the bright yellow rainwear, and in between all that, the bicycle lamps and the DVDs of American films. Luckily she didn't ask me once during this whole night what I'd advise her to do—if what she and her husband have is enough or much too little, if she should be grateful or if she's being made ill by her patience, possibly to the point of getting cancer. Nonetheless, I did have some influence on her, yes, to the limited extent to which that was possible. Even when I said nothing, that was a reaction. And now that I think about it, amid all the fluctuations, which affected me too, I generally encouraged her to hold onto her marriage, if only because she'd be lonely either way, with or without him, but it would certainly make a difference for the children. And the novel I'll write will also lean more towards finding what the two lovers have in common after all, rather than exclaiming, 'Enough, just call it a day!'

Or will that just be my own impression, and you'll read the book completely differently? No, I don't think so. Some other novelist, if Jutta had told him exactly the same things, looked at him with the same tears and clung to him in the same way, would savour that little bit of desperation much longer, would put even more acerbic words in her mouth, would refrain from making the comical conciliatory, and would thus tell a much nastier story that left divorce as the only way out. Only the fact that I cling to love until the end hints at its possibility. Anyone who is unmarried, hasn't been married long enough or is actually happily married may shake their head at Jutta persisting in her unhappiness. They'll ask why she doesn't make a fresh start—if not with me, because that would be ridiculous as a plot on top of everything else, then with the bishop, who would otherwise have been introduced for nothing. They'll assume that the reluctance to separate has something to do with my own trauma,

Maybe it's true that I'm biased. But the novel I'll write also follows a literature that certainly didn't make the case for infidelity, even if it expresses a longing in a way that still resonates today. It's just the floor, as I say, and it looks chaotic, with the shoes carelessly strewn on the floor, just as Jutta demonstrated. And yet every object tells a story that belongs to another: the ball that rolled against the doctor's bag, the running shoes of different sizes covered with the same mud, Jutta's elegant coat, hung over her husband's red all-weather jacket as if in an embrace.

That's the last thing I needed now, a rhyme in Gothic script above the toilet: 'The gentleman who sits to pee / will bring the housewife greater glee'. I expect Jutta had the enamel plaque custom-made because she found it original to combine this emancipatory command with old-fashioned language. The rhyme is more at her literary level than Proust, at any rate. And, in case I took it as a joke, there's also a diagram informing me of the expected posture: a standing stick man with a dotted line extending from his private parts into the toilet and splashing all over the place from there is crossed out in red; next to him, a sitting stick man whose aim stays within the toilet bowl is assigned a green tick. Jutta also installed a surveillance camera to be on the safe side, I groan inwardly, and even look around. And if a single drop should touch the ground, I'll be put straight by electric shocks.

God, how this forced equality gets on my nerves, already in Brokdorf, when the men even squatted in the fields out of solidarity with the women. At the same time, in this double appeal to one's personal conscience in a place where one definitely won't be seen, I detect a very unpleasant return of the kind of religion that was dominant around my home town. I'd love to scream into the living room that this is precisely the ethics that led to capitalism, yes, precisely your bloody Protestantism, because it turns humans into slaves who function without a master. Even in your sex life you're geared towards self-optimization, Jutta. That, exactly that and nothing else is the connection that leads to your work group. 'Work group'—that says it all. Instead of electric cars and solar panels, how much more subversive it would be in a thoroughly economized system to take a more relaxed view of things.

As always, the counterarguments immediately come to mind; I don't even have to think of climate change, which objectively calls for self-limitation and personal responsibility, only to picture the cleaning lady—no doubt one with a headscarf, as Jutta's so open-minded—who'll have to wipe up my urine. I also want to end the evening on a decent note, not have Jutta discover some droplets next to the toilet or on the rim of the bowl. The idea of a surveillance camera is obviously exaggerated—that would be totalitarian, totalitarian egalitarianism; but I wouldn't put it past Jutta to lift the seat and check. Back in the squat she already thought she had a monopoly on goodness, with much too much passion. What's more, I'm almost wobbling from fatigue as I unbutton my trousers. Well, that's how I find myself sitting down to pee for the first time in 30 years.

My editor will complain that I can't possibly have seen the rhyme in the toilet for the first time at five in the morning—with all the tea I would have drunk, as well as the weak bladder that's infamous among men my age.

'Maybe the house has several toilets,' I will say in another attempt to evade his criticism.

He'll lean over the desk with the manuscript on it and admit, with a suspicious smile, that such a large house undoubtedly has more than one toilet.

'Well, then everything's fine,' I will mumble and quickly move my index finger down to the next paragraph.

Then he'll press all five of his sausage fingers onto the previous paragraph and ask severely where, in my opinion, the second toilet is located.

'How should I know?' I will groan, 'On the first floor?'

So it's precisely where the children sleep and Jutta's husband may still be working—the editor won't have to say any more to convey to me, once again, what moments of suspense, I've denied the novelist by not going upstairs throughout the evening, creeping barefoot past mysterious doors until I reach the toilet, but then I knock against a chair in my clumsiness and someone wakes up—one of the children, her husband?—and one of the doors . . .

'You've left a grease stain again!' I will scold him, 'Five grease stains!' And I'll explain that letting obvious opportunities pass without taking them is precisely the thrill.

Then the editor will lean back into his movable backrest and sigh that I do what I want anyway; fortunately there are only a few pages left, and he hasn't noticed much of the thrill so far.

'You've been saying that since my first book!' I remind the editor, and then, to my own surprise, I pay him the ultimate compliment: 'I have no better reader than you.'

'It's just my job.'

As I aim deep into the toilet bowl, I wonder where my sudden anger came from before when I railed against the weighing up of pros and cons: was I angry because Jutta had spoken for hours without reaching any conclusion, or because she only needed me as a listener—a good friend, as women say when they're not at all interested in a man? I was angry more at myself, because I noticed even as I spoke that Jutta couldn't understand any of what I was trying to say. Not even in the novel I will write can I precisely grasp the thought, which is perhaps more of a feeling, a part of my experience. It's no consolation that novelists have always felt unable to match the novels written generations earlier, or simply other arts in their own time. Even Proust felt this when he wove Racine and *One Thousand and One Nights* into *Lost Time*, paid homage to Debussy and Monet; it was only after him that people were no longer deceived. 'It is so natural to be harsh and devious towards something one loves,' he knew, and also knew that malice is not aroused by indifference. After the initial infatuation, it is certainly rare for love to feel requited for years in the same way, not too much or too little. 'The beloved person is first the sickness and then the cure, which stops the sickness and thus only makes it worse.' Proust describes precisely the fluctuation between declarations of love and the desire for separation that Jutta has indulged in throughout the evening, because of the rhythmic succession of opposing movements, as the best way to tie the knot that becomes unbreakable. And it is indeed logical, as he notes at the height of his crisis with Albertine, that one rarely separates on good terms, for if one were 'on good terms', there would be no need to separate.

There must be divorces, especially without children, but supposedly with children too, that are amicable; one constantly reads about them in the glossy magazines—or, to be precise, the press releases of some management: joint childcare, deep respect, staying friends and so forth. Alright, I think to myself every time, maybe they weren't together for long, or maybe it was more of a public relationship, like Luise's parents in the Paris salons of old, except now in the jet set. But Proust isn't referring to such urbanity; he means the claustrophobic coexistence that love only achieved with modernity, where two people share everything—evenings, a bed, weekends, travels, friends, interests, now also parenting and housework—and infidelity is out of the question. After all, the volume about Albertine is entitled *The Prisoner* and the one without her *The Fugitive*.

> What attaches us to other human beings is the thousand tiny roots, the innumerable threads formed by memories of the previous evening, hopes for the following morning; it is this continuous web of habit from which we cannot extricate ourselves. Just as there are misers who pile up wealth from generous motives, we are prodigals who spend from avarice, and we sacrifice our lives not so much to a particular human being, but to all the sum of our hours, our days that he has managed to accrete around himself, everything in comparison with which

the life we have still to live, the relatively future life, seems to us a life more distant, more detached, less close to us, less ours. What we would need to do would be to break these bonds which are so much more important to us than he is, but they have the effect of creating in us a transient sense of obligation to him; we feel obliged not to leave him for fear of incurring his displeasure, whereas later we would do so, since then, detached from us, he would no longer be us; in reality, we are only creating obligations (even if, paradoxically, they drive us to suicide) towards ourselves.

The reader may still find it unconvincing that a substantial part of the novel I'll write consists of quotations. In a further attempt to explain, I will say that it's my way of declaring how much I need the books on my shelf. Perhaps I'm less concerned with Jutta than with the literature I love.

'I still don't entirely understand what you meant with the pros and cons,' Jutta will sigh when she reads the novel, and accuse me of simply using her marriage to write whatever I wanted to write about marriage anyway: 'And even if toilet rhymes are your idea of my literary level—thanks for that, by the way—the stuff with Albertine is something completely different.'

'Maybe,' I will reply, and admit that novelists are not reporters; in the end they always speak through the people they bring on stage, and don't give them those strange names so that their models won't be recognized, but because they really are different people, even if none of the readers believe it.

'But why do you have to use me at all?'

'I don't use you.'

'Yes you do, you use me.'

Maybe the friendship—I no longer dare to call it love—that will connect us in future despite, or rather with, all the little glitches and misunderstandings of our reunion; maybe her friendship will prove itself precisely in the fact that she allows the publication of the novel, even though I only made a few changes and left out as little as possible. Or is it compensation for the pain she caused me 30 years ago?

'I think it's more of a sense of gratitude,' Jutta will say, noting the loyalty I showed her for 30 long years. 'You took me in your arms . . . that was good for me. You can't imagine how much good it did me in that situation.'

She'll immediately adopt her emphatically grown-up, ironically schoolmarmish tone again, which is enough to take me back 30 years:

'A friend wouldn't do that.'

'What?'

'A novel like that.'

Because, in her little town at least, she's sure to be recognized after the next reading, even though she's not really Jutta.

When I return to the living room I find Jutta bent over, head in hands. Her upper body is rocking back and forth almost imperceptibly, as if she were whimpering quietly to herself. I ask if everything is alright, and when she doesn't respond I step towards the armchair. She looks up at me, smiling, and only now do I notice the smartphone in her lap and the two cables running across her neckline. She takes one of the earphones out of her ear and holds it out to me wordlessly, moving over slightly. I can't put my finger on the song but I recognize a sound that's so familiar to me, the naked sound of rock 'n' roll. I quickly squeeze next to her into the armchair, which seems to have gained exactly one backside's breadth, and put the earphone in my ear. That can't be, I tell myself over and over again, I'm dreaming, I must be dreaming; but there she is, there's Jutta, and I'm listening to 'Ramada Inn' with her: such beautiful, such poignant music. It's also strange that although I'm only listening with one earphone, all four instruments are clear in the mix. I don't understand and begin reaching over to touch my other ear, but I find Jutta's head leaning there and certainly don't want to drive it away. Moving my upper body back and forth in synch with hers, I get into the rhythm, which is not fast, never fast, and feel the fundamental tone of life itself, with the two guitars in between like a married couple on a long drive. I'd really like to know if Jutta feels the same, this moment of agreement, indeed an affirmation of everything, in spite of how everything turned out, if she feels exactly the same way as I do—whether such simultaneity, an almost electric emotional connection, actually exists. And then Jutta's husband is standing at the door.

I will almost have finished writing the novel by the time I open the booklet to look up the lines I can't make out. First I'll be surprised that the lyrics are even shorter than they sound: three sparse verses and a chorus, which take no more than a minute to read even though the song is over 20 minutes long—that one can portray an entire marriage in so few words if one has the music to go with it. Then I realize that it's not just any marriage: the husband's an alcoholic. 'Had a few drinks and now they're feeling fine', we already heard in the second verse, but only now do I understand why his wife doesn't recognize him in the third verse: because he's totally plastered. 'He just looks away and checks out', whatever 'checks out' means here. And only after he's looked away, not before that, only then does she plead with him, as she's done who knows how many times before, that 'it's time to do something'. That's why she mentions the friends; I finally understand now, despite the American accent and the delivery: 'Maybe talk to his old friends who gave it up'. But he just pours himself a 'tall one', closes his eyes and says that it's enough. Even those listeners whose English is better than mine will only realize at the end what the wife has tried so often, why she has cried so often.

At the end, with only two or three hints in the third verse that turn an ordinary marital row into an alcoholism drama, Neil Young shifts the song from the general to the specific and proves that Tolstoy was right: all unhappy marriages are unhappy in their own way. Who am I to claim otherwise?—though I'm still not convinced that all happy marriages are similar, but no one has to tell us about the happy ones anyway, assuming they actually exist. I'll continue to wonder, to wonder again and anew, while Neil Young sings the chorus for the last time, the rhythm returns and the guitars join the motorway: what does he mean by 'that's enough', since the couple are just carrying on with what they have to do, what they need? That it's enough of the alcohol, that he pours himself a final 'tall one' and resolves for the umpteenth time to stop? Or enough of her warnings, enough of 'where are we stopping, I need a pee, when are we getting something to eat?' Enough of the silence at supper, enough crying, in the hotel bed too shortly, enough of this marriage, which has driven him to addiction and her to despair? But they love each other so.

By now I've forgotten how we got onto the subject, but I suddenly find myself having a discussion with Jutta about the sonic impoverishment resulting from MP3 and other digital formats. Well, strictly speaking we're not discussing any more; I'm insisting, almost shouting at her, that she can't possibly listen to Neil Young and Crazy Horse on her iPhone, because the formats that are normal now, which are admittedly convenient because of their compression, only contain five per cent of the original data. Because Jutta evidently doesn't understand, or doesn't want to—she just shakes her head—I try to explain it with the analogy of a digital photo with very low resolution: she wouldn't want to look at that, yet she doesn't care when it comes to music because her ear has got used to the coarsening of sound, because it is a coarsening, an impoverishment, Neil Young keeps saying it himself, which is why he's been on a crusade against MP3s and iTunes for years and enlisted a whole armada of audiophile technicians to develop his own player, Pono, which came so close to the original sound, which only analogue formats can capture, that even his ears couldn't tell the difference. And what happens? Jutta's husband, who is by no means as tall and athletic as I imagined him, not blonde either, and seems more like a nerd, a computer- or book-lover with deathly pale skin, deep rings under his eyes, hanging shoulders and thin, shoulder-length hair, evidently a chain-smoker too, judging by how deeply he draws on the cigarette he's holding between his middle and ring fingers—Jutta's husband agrees with me emphatically that one should never listen to music, real music at least, on an iPhone: it's barbaric, far removed from real experience. It's a slightly strange situation: the sun is already rising outside and the two of us are standing in front of Jutta, agreeing that one wouldn't look at a Vermeer on a phone screen either, after all; not only because the screen is small, but because it's flat, pure surface, a smooth, shiny surface. But Jutta doesn't want to hear it; she stares stubbornly at her iPhone and sinks into her armchair. We should change the subject, I think to myself, things are starting to get unpleasant. For Jutta, they evidently got unpleasant some time ago.

'Listening to an MP3 is like being stuck at the bottom of the sea with heavy diving gear,' Jutta's husband states, attempting an explanation that I've heard somewhere before. 'You get a bit higher with a CD, but it's only at 192 kilohertz that you break through the surface of the water and can breathe the air.'

'Yes,' I agree, but only because I remember the number; it was in an article, an interview or something similar. '192 kilohertz, anything else is useless.'

No longer facing Jutta at all, Jutta's husband reports that even Steve Jobs listened exclusively to vinyl at home; that already shows how mendacious the system is. As I nod at him, I wonder what she could possibly find attractive about him. She declared that her marriage is sexually stable, after all, complaining in the same breath how fanatically he does sports— indeed, he has to, so as to stay attractive. But this man here,

Jutta's husband, really doesn't look like someone engaged in self-optimization. Even his teeth don't look well-groomed; behind the cracked lips, probably a result of all the smoking, I see a brown shimmer. Am I crazy, or does love really make people so blind? Anyway, I'm always pleased to find someone who shares my enthusiasm about Neil Young, and I bend down to Jutta again and try to convey to her that the sense of depth we attribute to the music and feel subjectively as warmth, this truly physically palpable element at a live concert—vibrating, stroking, caressing, droning—that it's produced by the tiny overtones which bring everything together and create the sonic landscape in 'Ramada Inn', that specific Crazy Horse sound. Jutta starts crying, covers her ears as the two of us go on and on, and tells us to leave her alone, she just wanted to listen to a song. Then she throws the iPhone on the floor along with the earphones and runs out of the living room. We have to start with the young, I call after her, it's a matter for the schools, a matter of education, to prevent the senses from being dulled in the digital age.

'Everything alright?'

'What?'

'Is everything alright?'

I hear a knock—no, a banging, someone's banging on the door. What door? I look around and find myself sitting on a toilet. What toilet?

'Hello!'

That's Jutta's voice, oh God, and it's her toilet I'm sitting on, Jutta's guest toilet, with my trousers around my ankles.

I leap up to check if I've made the floor dirty and lift the toilet lid. Not a drop anywhere, luckily. I quickly pull up my trousers, flush the toilet and wash my hands. Relieved that things didn't turn out worse, I open the door and see Jutta standing in the hallway, the smudged mascara now wiped away; she looks as if she's generally tidied herself up.

'Did you fall asleep or what?' she asks, with the smile that already brought me to my knees as a 15-year-old, her cheeks round and glowing like two apricots.

'All because I had to sit down to pee.'

Then her cheeks flatten a little as she opens her mouth. Am I still dreaming or am I awake, I ask myself as the gap in her teeth comes into view.

# TRANSLATOR'S NOTES

Quotations are taken from the following books:

ADORNO, Theodor W. *Minima Moralia: Reflections on a Damaged Life* (Edmund Jephcott trans.). London and New York: Verso, 2005.

BALZAC, Honoré de. *The Girl with the Golden Eyes* (Peter Collier trans.). Oxford and New York: Oxford University Press, 2012.

———. *The Memoirs of Two Young Wives* (Jordan Stump trans.). New York: New York Review of Books, 2018.

BERNANOS, Georges. *Diary of a Country Priest* (Howard Curtis trans.). London: Penguin, 2019.

DUMAS, Alexandre, *fils*. *The Lady of the Camellias* (Liesl Schillinger trans.) London: Penguin, 2013.

FLAUBERT, Gustave. *Madame Bovary* (Margaret Mauldon trans.). Oxford and New York: Oxford University Press, 2004.

GREEN, Julien. *Adrienne Mesurat* (Henry Longan Stuart trans.). New York: Holmes and Meier, 1991.

KUNDERA, Milan. *Immortality* (Peter Kussi trans.). London: Faber & Faber, 2001.

MAUPASSANT, Guy de. *A Parisian Affair and Other Stories* (Siân Miles trans.). London: Penguin, 2004.

PROUST, Marcel. *Finding Time Again* (Ian Patterson trans.). London: Penguin, 2003.

——. *The Guermantes Way* (Mark Treharne trans.). London: Penguin, 2003.

——. *In the Shadow of Young Girls in Flower* (James Grieve trans.). London: Penguin, 2003.

——. *The Prisoner and the Fugitive* (Carol Clark and Peter Collier trans). London: Penguin, 2003.

——. *Sodom and Gomorrah* (John Sturrock trans.). London: Penguin, 2003.

——. *Swann's Way* (Lydia Davis trans.). London: Penguin, 2003.

STENDHAL. *On Love* (Sophie Lewis trans.). London: Hesperus, 2009.

——. *The Red and the Black* (Roger Gard trans.). London: Penguin, 2002.

ZOLA, Émile. *Thérèse Raquin* (Robin Buss trans.). London: Penguin, 2004.

The three essays referred to in the novel are the following:

KALKA, Joachim. 'Proust und die Affaire Dreyfus'. *Jahrbuch des Simon-Dubnow-Instituts* (14) (2015).

LAURIN, Stefan. 'Die große Ernüchterung. Ökoautoritäres Denken greift um sich—und hat einen Klassenfeind: das Proletariat'. *K-West, Magazin für Kunst, Kultur und Gesellschaft* (5) (2015).

MAAR, Michael. 'Spargel mit Fissuren' in *Prousts Pharao*. Berlin: Berenberg, 2009.